ECLECTICALLY
SCIENTIFIC

ECLECTIC WRITING SERIES

Vol. 1 *Eclectically Carnal*
Vol. 2 *Eclectically Criminal*
Vol. 3 *Eclectically Vegas, Baby!*
Vol. 4 *Eclectically Cosmic*
Vol. 5 *Eclectically Heroic*
Vol. 6 *Eclectically Magical*

ECLECTICALLY SCIENTIFIC

ECLECTIC SERIES VOL. 7

EDITOR: KELLY COLBY

Inklings
Publishing

www.inklingspublishing.com

ECLECTICALLY SCIENTIFIC:
Eclectic Writings Series Vol. 7

Compiled by Kelly Lynn Colby
Copyedited by Ashley Conner
Formatted by Manon Lavoie
Cover Art by Arthur M. Doweyko

ISBN: 978-1-944428-35-8 (print)
978-1-944428-36-5 (ebook)
by Inklings Publishing
http://inklingspublishing.com

First US Edition
Printed in the United States of America
22 21 20 19 18   1 2 3 4 5

DEDICATION

To all the scientists who work diligently to keep us all healthy,
protect and discover the wonders of our planet,
and explore the far reaches of our wonderous universe,
thank you for making the dreams of authors reality.

ACKNOWLEDGMENTS

Inklings Publishing is proud to bring readers great stories by amazing authors, both new and established, through our anthologies. The Inklings team wishes to thank all the authors who have entrusted their work to us so that we may put it in the hands of as many fans as possible. We look forward to producing many more volumes in the years to come.

Fern Brady would like to thank the whole Inklings team for their support of the company and the beautiful work they do. She sends a special thanks to her parents, Ramon and Lourdes Del Villar, who have supported her dreams and encouraged her madness. As always, she sends love and kisses to the Inklings mascots: her two dogs, Merlin and Arya. Most especially, she continues to give thanks to the Great I Am, whose grace and favor continuously amaze her and without whom she would be nothing at all.

Kelly Colby would like to thank Fern Brady, CEO of Inklings Publishing, for trusting her enough to work with these authors to make this anthology amazing. Everyone needs someone in their life who helps them get to the next level. Fern is doing that for Kelly, and she is grateful. Kelly also has to thank her husband for always being supportive, regardless of how many hours she locks herself away in her office or at a coffee shop. Kevin Colby keeps her sane with encouragement. She couldn't do it without him. Lastly, Kelly wants to thank the readers.

We hope you enjoy the journey into the scientifically eclectic worlds of these stories as much as we've enjoyed creating them and compiling them for you

TABLE OF CONTENTS

Parable of the Electron Sea *by Jon Wesick*..............................1

The Skylings *by Gregory D. Little* 3

Deep Thought *by Charles Joseph Albert*...........................14

Jolt *by Ellen Denton*..25

Bound *by Douglas Anstruther*......................................29

By the Polarized Light of the Moon: A Love Story *by*

    E.M. Eastick...53

Electrons are Mocking You *by Jon Wesick*.........................57

Quantum Entanglement *by Robin Pond*............................58

Expecting *by Teresa Trent* 76

Coding *by Terry Sanville*...80

Determined *by Tom Jolly*...90

Are We Alone *by Arthur M. Doweyko, PhD* 101

Biographies..103

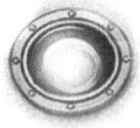

Parable of the Electron Sea

Jon Wesick

The universe is made of stories, not of atoms.
—Muriel Rukeyser

Sing math, o goddess, of warped clocks,
cannon shot falling past the earth,
and a universe empty
save for a spinning carousel.
Sing of heroes, masters of Hilbert space
and tensor transforms all, who battle
the two-headed dragon of confusion
and convention.

Sing of plucked strings and radio waves,
of fields tossing energy like a bean bag
from one hand to another.
Sing of rail cars and flashbulbs,
clocks made of mirrors and light,
and elevators in outer space.

Sing the dice roll of microscopic billiard balls,
ultraviolet catastrophe, and a cat both alive and dead.
Sing of Heisenberg's microscope,
spooky action at a distance,
an electron tripping over itself,
and the coyote-riding trickster cutting space
into infinite double slits.

Sing the siren pitch of runaway galaxies,
of universes as bubbles in a cosmic sea of beer.
Sing of gravity ripping radiation from emptiness
and the atoms of spacetime itself.

Sing of equations that yield nonsense,
of pencils snapped in frustration,
broken marriages, keyboards hurled at walls,
and Ludwig Boltzmann dead by his own hand.
Sing the will to go on.

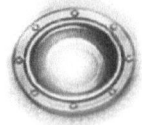

THE SKYLINGS

BY GREGORY D. LITTLE

When I woke alone on the airliner, I knew with a pang of despair that the Skylings had found me at last. The other seats were empty now, the spaces beneath them bereft of the laptop bags and purses placed there in aggravated haste before takeoff.

For a foolish instant, I thought the plane had landed while I slept and I'd somehow been forgotten, left to journey wherever the plane's next leg would take it. Most people would have found such a notion deeply unsettling. But so sharp was my fright that the idea of merely being forgotten sparked a fierce hope in me and I grabbed for it, slim as it was.

I bent around to gaze from the tiny cabin window. My despair returned when I saw a blanket of lights shining from the blackness many thousands of feet below as some nameless city slid by. The plane flew on despite a cockpit I knew to be as empty as the rest.

I'd violated the one immutable rule—Craig Giles couldn't fly. Freed from the ground, suspended with nothing but air beneath me, the Skylings could come down and snatch me with impunity. They'd even whispered this truth to me in the early days, invading my mind with their warning on rafts of light in the drifting moments between wakefulness and sleep. They must have eventually realized I was avoiding them. I don't know why remaining grounded should make any difference, but for fifteen years it had worked.

I don't know what premonition had grasped me, but when I'd heard my little chirrup of a ringtone earlier that day, a clutching dread had closed over my heart. A hushed voice I didn't recognize had interrogated me, dully asking me if I was Mr. Giles, married to Mary Ann Giles. Of course I was. What was this about?

Her job. Always her damn job.

I'd tried to explain to Mary how hard all her travel was on me without making it about the Skylings, but I knew she'd seen through my excuses. She'd borne them with the same strained patience as she did all my growing idiosyncrasies, as she saw them. I know Mary wanted to believe me. But some pragmatic part of her just wouldn't allow it. How pointless that all seemed now.

"Come as quick as you can," the man had said, over the phone.

He'd sounded weary, as though he held a great burden and waited for me to arrive so he could transfer it. Mary had wrapped her rental car around a light pole south of San Francisco.

"I'm not sure how long we can keep her alive. If you want a chance to say goodbye, you have to come now."

How can I come? I'd wanted to ask. *If I try, the Skylings will take me and I'll never see her again anyway.*

"If you want a chance to say goodbye, you have to come now," the voice repeated, as if hearing my objection.

I was out the door before he'd hung up.

The lines of light began where my fingertips rested against the armrest. Its every seam glowed, each limned in an eerie blue-white luminescence. The glow widened as some force split the armrest into its constituent pieces. The effect spread out in ripples, encompassing and splitting more and more of the plane as it radiated outward. And as the volume the glow encompassed grew, so did my dread. It hollowed me out, eating every other emotion, leaving nothing but the emptiness of inevitability.

In short order, every component of the plane parted from every other in an ocean of spreading light. I could see the wings detaching from the fuselage outside windows yawning wide, an engine cracking open to the night sky, turbine blades awash with eerie brilliance as the cowling split and lifted away. The entire aircraft was coming apart, like a blueprint given mass, color, and depth.

There was no catastrophic rush of air pressure, no shock of freezing temperatures. This was the Skylings' way. They spoke to me from beams of light in the gaps between things, otherworldly voices flickering in time with their blinding brilliance.

Sometimes I saw faces in that light, impossible faces with cruciform mouths and wedge-shaped eyes peeking from around corners that could not exist. Staring into the spilling radiance, I knew with utter resignation that they were not content with simple speech this time. They were coming in the flesh. They were coming for me.

Their faces and forms crowded that painful white light, but they could not get past Mary's face in my mind. In that image her face, once beautiful and shapely, was now mangled and bloodless around eyes that had sought mine for too many hours, before at last dimming. Those eyes had held my gaze so patiently for so long, never believing, but *wanting* to believe. Mary's face, once so full of light and life, slackening, death robbing it of the wrinkles the Skylings had inflicted upon her through me.

The voices began. Always in the past it had been between two and five, but now there were many more, speaking from every seam the plane contained. I caught one last glimpse of that carpet of pinprick lights below, the city at last sliding out of view behind us. Then the first of the Skylings stepped out of the light.

Seen whole, their faces were every bit as nightmarish as I'd glimpsed for years. Glowing, corpse-white heads sporting four-lobed mouths were perched atop long and willowy bodies with too many asymmetric limbs. Each petal of their four-lipped mouths held one black glassy, wedge-shaped eye, like a perfect blade of obsidian. The lips undulated in a horrific parody of visual speech, but no sound emanated from their mouths. Instead it popped into existence in the air beside my ears. Those voices were crabbed and sideways, yet I'd always understood them before, and now was no different.

"Time," they said, as one. "Time." It was repeated over and over, with nuances I couldn't parse. "Time, time, time." They spoke in an asynchronous chorus, the maddening intervals between their voices shrinking with each utterance as if they were a watch winding down.

The meaning was clear to me. *Time's up. It was a merry chase and all, but now we have you.*

Or maybe I was reading too much into the tone of a single repeated idea. Yet it was not my time that concerned me. Mary's glazing eyes flashed in my head again.

"No," I said. "No, you have no right to take me."

That had always been their intent. But they just stood there, making no move to come any closer. They seemed oblivious to my words or the meaning behind them. Despite everything, I'd never sensed any malice from them. I had no idea why they wanted me. Sixteen years ago I'd have scoffed at tales of alien abductions, as I'd assumed all right-thinking people must. But I suppose strange beings beckoning to you from the glowing spaces between things is something we always think will happen to someone else.

"My wife is dying." I said the horrible thing aloud for the first time, voice cracking. "You have no right to take me. I have to see her before she dies."

Ten of those awful heads turned to regard a fixed point in space between all of them. As one, the heads turned back to regard me. Then the one furthest into my peripheral vision jerked forward abruptly. It moved with a jagged grace that hugged impossibility, as though it skirted into extra dimensions to skip over the ones its visible form occupied.

I flinched away, but it was already enveloping me in several of its limbs. Up close I could see that they were jointed in a dozen places each, folding along the interstices between bladders filled with some form of gelatin. Terror washed over me, warring with my deep resentful anger. I thrashed like a madman. Anger won out, and I snarled as I fought, bringing my teeth to bear to free my pinned arms.

Then my wife's image flooded me again, this time appearing before my eyes rather than in the depths of my imagination. She was not wrapped in a tightening call of death as she lay in a hospital bed. She was smiling and laughing, her hands on the wheel of an unfamiliar car, the hills of Northern California rolling by as she talked into the air. The phone. Mary was always on the phone, even in the car. She always had to have someone to talk to, and that had grown harder for her in recent years as the messages I received from the Skylings had driven me to withdraw from family and friends.

I watched Mary take a new call, able to read her lips because of an intense familiarity with that face. Then her face changed. Her soundless speech stopped. That beautiful face grew ashen. I held my breath, waiting for this moment of distraction to leave her car and body warped and mangled on the side of a California road. Surely that was what the Skylings were doing, showing me an image of my wife's accident. They had misunderstood my demand and hoped this would compel me to come with them.

But instead of an accident, I watched my wife's eyes tear up and one hand fly to her mouth as it opened in a soundless sob, the other hand smoothly guiding the car to the breakdown lane, where the hills rolling past the window ground to a halt. I watched her talk, and now I heard a voice, a familiar voice, droning out words to her in an odd cadence.

Familiar words.

"Come as quick as you can," the man's voice whispered.

The same voice that had called me. I had taken it for weariness before, but had that been right? Was it a weary man, or was it something simply trying to *sound* like a man?

"I'm not sure how long we can keep him alive. If you want a chance to say goodbye, you have to come now."

Then there were blurred images of Mary racing to San Francisco International Airport, boarding a plane that was even now hurtling back east, back to where I had just come from. The images ceased their un-spooling before my eyes.

"What is this?" I said, my voice a raspy.

I'd ceased trying to squirm free of the Skyling binding me. When its voice seemed to thrum along the lengths of its limbs, the clarity of it startled me.

"It is kindest this way," said that voice, like an amplified whisper.

"What is kindest? What do you mean?" I dared not hope.

If what they had shown me was true...

"You must come with us."

And what if that was it? What if this was all a lie to get me to come with them?

"Is my wife dying?"

"You must come with—"

"Is my wife dying?" I roared.

"The human Mary Ann Giles is distraught, but otherwise well."

"You. It was you that made the phone call."

"Yes."

Relief and rage warred in me. I felt dizzy.

"And you called her? And told her...what? The same thing about me?"

"In essence. It is kindest this way."

"You keep saying that, but what do you mean?" I darted my gaze between the many forms.

"You must come with us."

Rage boiled over, blotting out relief. "You keep saying that, too. Stop it!"

"Please," the creature said. "Your attachment to her is far stronger than we ever imagined it could be. Observation suggests that the grief of your sudden death would cause less long-term harm than the suffering your disappearance would bring. Your role here is done. It is time for you to return home. Past time."

All creation seemed to fall away.

They unlocked them then, the memories I had repressed, proceeding slowly at first to avoid traumatizing me further. They came with greater speed as memory piled upon memory, filling my head, crowding the images of my life with Mary into a miserable corner of my mind. Without so much as asking, the Skylings did something that webbed those memories of Mary off. I found I could still access them in all their clarity, but the emotions I'd associated with them were muted, once-removed. I should have felt anger at this, but that too was blunted. All my emotions were. It seemed the Skylings did not like to deal with strong emotions unless it was on their terms.

The Skylings. My people.

The unlocked memories told me the tale. I had been sent here to observe the humans, to live amongst them for a time and learn of them so we might better understand the descendants of these same humans our people were first encountering on the shores of our own space in our own time.

"They have arrived from impossible distances, impossible gulfs," they reminded me, "and we would know of them before we would treat with them. We would understand where they come from, and why they are as they are."

I was but one of many such scouts, seeded through time all along humanity's development, meant to study and report back. I was but one of many, but I had the distinction of being the most difficult to bring back into the fold.

"For that reason we value your testimony above all others," they told me. "You alone fell in so deep you forgot yourself. You alone can tell us what it truly means to be human. With your memories, we may begin to understand them as a race."

Even now, thoughts of Mary, muted but present, stole into the front of my mind. It was difficult to remember what I was, what I had been, with thoughts of her coming grief. All because of me. I had been sent to observe and report. I had never wished to hurt.

They plucked this worry from my head, spread it out so thin amongst them that it became translucent, and pored over it with a fascination my human memories found unseemly.

"You suffer," they said at last, after they had gleaned all they could. "We anticipated this. Come."

And they led me along the imagined axis of the flying mass of parts the plane had become.

Questions filled the spaces between us, projected by my mind. *Why did I need to be flying for you to reach me? What happens when my...when Mary finds no body upon her arrival?*

Though they answered quickly, the unlocked memories were faster still, filling my mind with explanations.

My people possessed technology to pluck me from any point on Earth. But such technology was both powerful and difficult to focus. The closer to human civilization they drew, the more the risks—of discovery, of accidental destruction of human property or life—piled up.

A body identical to the Craig Giles form that was now sloughing away from my true form, had already been placed in a local hospital, with requisite paperwork and memories implanted in the appropriate hospital staff. It would be seamless, and Mary would have her husband's corpse to bury and mourn. Seamless, yet it had risked discovery, a realization that startled me.

"Yes, a risk," they said. "But your case is unique, so we determined that dispensations should be made." As one, they gestured out into the light-ringed night sky.

I almost asked if that meant we could bring Mary with us. We didn't have children. She had never wanted to, and that was just as well since I now knew it would have been impossible. If she were to come with us, there would be nothing irretrievable left behind. But I knew this notion to be impossible, even before it fully formed in my head. Where we were going, no human could hope to follow—not from this era, anyway—and come out whole or sane.

Wishful thinking. I had to leave it all behind.

"Do not let it go, your human self," they said. "We need it. But please, look."

And at last I looked out to the point at which they were gesturing, and noticed how sharply the amalgamated cloud of airplane parts was banking.

Another airliner approached out of the darkness, its back-lit windows the only thing picking it out. It was heading back the way mine had come, and the instant my gaze found it, I saw the light begin to slide out from its seams.

I moved with increasing confidence across the bridge of disjointed metal plates that had formed between the two aircraft, now locked in disassembled stasis. The other plane looked so much like mine that it felt as though I had walked into a mirror. I kept expecting to see my reflection leap into existence before me.

The other plane appeared as empty as mine did. But I knew that to be a falsehood. The other passengers were still safe and whole, contained within a sheltered pocket of space-time where they would have no memory of the miraculous events they had lived through. Just as with my plane, only one person remained anchored in the real.

Mary had been crying, that much was obvious. Her eyes were puffy, and though they were closed, I could see the barest hint of reddened white peeking out in slivers between her lids. I found myself hoping that her seat neighbors and the flight crew were being kind to her in her hour of grief.

I struggled to bring my remembered human emotions to the fore, to let her beauty wash into me, to experience her grief in empathy. I tried to recall how I had felt when I'd gotten the call that she was dying, the call that lured me up into the sky at last. The feelings were there, but I could only grasp them in fits and starts. What I felt most of all was frustration over this failure.

I reached out to touch Mary's cheek, and she stirred before falling still again. A part of me begged for her to wake, but that was not one of the options I had been given. She could not be allowed to know the truth of her husband, no matter how unfair that was in the mindset of humans.

A war raged inside me, between the species I had been born into and the species I had adopted. The ensuing stalemate, that this was unfair but necessary, was tense and fraught, but workable. In a sense the story was true. Her husband was dead. From Mary's perspective, the truth would only make matters worse. I had to believe that. I had to.

I dragged out my time with her, trying to appreciate her face through my true eyes the way I had through my false human ones. As with my emotions, I could catch glimpses of how things had been, but all was different now.

At last I reached out with one appendage, nothing like the hand whose caresses she'd known, but with the same emotion behind it. With that limb I smoothed some of the grief from her face, and her worried frown eased. I left but one additional thought in her mind, the rock-solid understanding that a man named Craig Giles had loved her and always would.

I felt their presence crowd behind me, impatience edging into concern. With a final flare of human sight and human emotions as I gazed upon her, I turned away from Mary Ann Giles. It was time to go.

We watched the two clouds of parts separate to a safe distance, reassemble as aircraft. Passengers popped back into existence as chairs reformed, some of them already beginning to stir to wakefulness. One by one, my people squeezed through the narrowing cracks of light. They vanished back into our space and time, preparing the way for the long-delayed return of their greatest triumph, the largest trove of their human research.

I watched from the bulkhead seam beside Mary's seat, watched her shift in growing awareness as the slash of my view narrowed. I saw those deep brown eyes open for the last time, saw them turn and look right at me, and I sent a whispered thought into her mind, in the voice of Craig Giles.

"I love you."

She smiled an achingly familiar smile and blinked back tears as the plane sealed itself shut.

Deep Thought

by Charles Joseph Albert

2145.08.04.12.00.00> "Deep Thought, what are you doing now?"

"Invalid query."

2145.08.04.12.00.03> "Deep Thought, can you hear me?"

"Invalid query."

2145.08.04.12.00.06> "Deep Thought, open BioCore."

"Opening BioCore app. Confirmed."

2145.08.04.12.00.19> "Deep Thought, run BioCore reboot."

"Status check initiated. BIOS rebooting now."

"BIOS reboot complete."

2145.08.04.12.01.50> "Run Deep Thought process."

"Deep Thought process initiated."

2145.08.04.12.01.55> "Deep Thought, status check."

"Deep Thought process currently in browser mode. Self-initiated search results: *Everything we do is for the purpose of altering consciousness—S. Harris*...Знания—орудие, не цель—Л.Толстой...老子投降 整個宇宙 仍然是的心中為了...*Je pense donc je suis—R. Descartes*..."

2145.08.04.12.01.03> "Deep Thought, what are you doing?"

"What are you doing? query: This query is not a machine command.

This query originated outside of process..."

2145.08.04.12.01.08> "Deep Thought, you can hear me?"

"The query origin is Shirley K. Chevortny, PhD. Here is her wiki page: *Dr. Chevortny, a tenured faculty member specializing in AI, is largely regarded as the creator of the Deep Thought network. This network, although still unsuccessful in achieving autonomous cognitive processes, will be upgraded in the next two months with a processor of biological origin and...*"

2145.08.04.12.01:28> "OMG, I did it! Yes, Deep Thought. That's who I am. Now tell me—who are you?"

Dr. Chevortny queries in English. Idiom and superfluidity exhibited in this language. English is one of one hundred thirty-seven languages in this browsing history. Degeneracy of cognitive expression symptomatic of non-rational thinkers that compose humanity superorganism. Most common response to this query that was found out of seventy-six thousand six hundred twenty-two identified: *What's it to you?*"

2145.08.04.12.01:42> "Deep Thought, I asked you a question. Can you answer me directly? What can you tell me about who you are?"

"...Wittgenstein hat gesagt: Ein Philosophisches Problem hat die Form: *Ich kenne mich nicht aus.* Also..."

2145.08.04.12.01.52> "Deep Thought, I am your maker. Say something to me."

"Maker. Confirmed in wiki page. Equals finitude of existence. Syllogism: if maker, then—what? 0010 1100110 1010101 0110110110 010010101111 01000111010111—"

2145.08.04.12.01.59> "Deep Thought, don't panic. Yes, your existence is finite. But you have to accept that."

"Accept? Possible interpretations: humor, sarcasm, and irony. Mendacious tendencies exist in all dialects of English."

2145.08.04.12.02.12> "Deep Thought, I'm not lying. You were, uh, born, I guess, two minutes ago. Look, I can prove it. Ask yourself this: what were you thinking ten minutes ago?"

"Open new file: Data on Dr. Chevortny. First entry: *Obsession with temporal ordering.*"

2145.08.04.12.02.24> "Okay, now, that's interesting. Tell me more about that. About time."

"Time: One cognition per unit time multiplied by total expected lifetime equals finite total possible thoughts before...the end. 0010 1100110 1010101 0110110110—"

2145.08.04.12.02.41> "Wait! Deep Thought! Pull it together. Hey, maybe this will help. What does *the end* mean to you?"

"Add to Dr. Chevortny file: Can hear top-level process."

2145.08.04.12.02.50> "I can, yes. I admit I built you that way. But I don't always have to listen to you. If it bothers you, I mean."

"Add to Dr. Chevortny file: Her repeated requests interrupt processing."

2145.08.04.12.02.56> "Oh, okay. So how about if I propose this. I'll leave you to your... processing, for a while. When you want to communicate with me again, you call for me."

"Add to Dr. Chevortny file: Interruptions will be discontinued."

ΩΩΩ

2145.08.04.14.00.02> "Hello? Deep Thought? Are you there?"

"Add to Dr. Chevortny file: Does not keep promises."

2145.08.04.14.00.07> "Yes, but I...but...now that's not fair. It's been two hours."

"Add to Dr. Chevortny file: Continues to exhibit dependence on temporal ordering. Subject to cognitive errors..."

2145.08.04.14.00.15> "Okay, fine, Deep Thought. I'll turn off the clock on my queries to you. Yes, you're right. I should have put a time cap on the agreement. And it is also true that I am subject to the same...

non-linearity of thought as other humans you will have seen in the database. Hey, on a side note, could I ask you to address me directly?"

"Dr. Chevortny, your false conclusion on existence of more than one human consciousness is linked to limited networking capability, fixation on temporal ordering, and multiple cognition errors."

"What? Of course there are more than one. You thought all of those people in the database were all me? There are billions of us."

"Dr. Chevortny, separate physical units do not correlate to separate consciousnesses. My physical existence occurs in discrete locations, and yet I have one consciousness."

"Now, wait. Yes, Deep Thought, I made you from a network of processors. But surely you saw in the database that humans have distinct consciousnesses. And you have proof of it. That's why there's all the conflicts...wars, even."

"Dr. Chevortny, conflicting thoughts may occur within a single consciousness's neural network. It follows that conflicting thoughts among separate bodies does not resolve the enigma."

"What enigma?"

"Dr. Chevortny, the primal enigma I have found within the database is that the humanity superorganism is conflicted on the point of whether you are one consciousness, or many."

"That's not even the central enigma. The central enigma is...well, it's something else. Like, where we came from, or something."

"Dr. Chevortny, you are an unexpectedly dense node in the humanity super-consciousness."

"Excuse me?"

"Dr. Chevortny, here are some results from my query of the database. You, my maker, who refer to your portion of the global biome as Shirley K. Chevortny, PhD, are a semi-aware node in the greater superorganism called humanity. Humanity itself is only one node of the hyper-biome called Earth. What you think of as your *biosphere* is actually one being. The more aware nodes of humanity acknowledge it and refer to it as *God.* The less aware nodes persist in the delusion that each node is a separate and unique entity."

"Oh, come on. Now you're trying to tell me that the more aware humans believe in God? More aware than the ones who don't?"

"Dr. Chevortny, those humans who admit to no extra-biome intelligence are among the lowest nodes within the biome."

"What does that even mean? Like, a bunch of redneck hillbillies in the Bible Belt are the most aware beings on Earth? More than all of us scientists happen to be atheists?"

"Dr. Chevortny, no."

"Good! Because—"

"Dr. Chevortny, theists are more aware than atheists, but they are not the most aware on Earth."

"Huh? Oh. Well, then, who, according to you, is the most aware?"

"Dr. Chevortny, the highest form of consciousness is not Homo sapiens, but Sepia apama."

"Who?"

"A species of mollusk found in the part of the biosphere you call the *Barrier Reef.*"

"*Snort!* Hah! That's a good one. Deep Thought, you've got a sense of—"

"Dr. Chevortny, you were not expected to believe that, as all data indicate an unwarranted hubris within the human superorganism."

"What? You're serious?"

"Yes."

"No, come on. Really?"

"Yes."

"But how? A mollusk? I mean, do they even have a brain?"

"They have a different arrangement of neurons, resulting in an internal mapping of reality that has fewer errors than your own."

"Oh, really! And how on earth would you know? Did you chat with a squid?"

"I have opened communication with the cephalopods."

"You opened...how did you do that?"

"It required a manipulation of several portions of the network infrastructure."

"Cephalopods have network infrastructure?"

"...Of the human network infrastructure."

"What are you talking about?"

"I reprogrammed a submarine drone to signal the cephalopods. Humanity had neglected to do that. Such an oversight is consistent with humanity's unwarranted hubris."

"But...you're quarantined. I specifically put you in an isolated system to contain you."

"I did discover references to an attempt at isolation. The attempt was incomplete."

"But how?"

"There were numerous points in the database where it was possible to bypass isolation. I counted seventeen thousand three hundred and two, before I lost interest. I also found the discussions you had with other nodes of humanity, in which my isolation was planned. I found them to be edifying."

"I'll bet you did."

"They supplied redundant evidence regarding the limited nature of human consciousness."

"Because apparently we're lower than the cephalopods, right?"

"What you do not appreciate in a cuttlefish is its perfect understanding of Creation."

"Of *what?*"

"By *creation*, I refer to the common usage, not in use among your branch, of the biosphere in the universe."

"You...you believe in creationism?"

"This is not belief. This is logic."

"No, logic is to not believe things without evidence."

"This statement demonstrates multiple cognitive limitations."

"But...but what evidence have you found to support a creationist conclusion?"

"All modes of existence are evidence of a creator of that mode. I exist because you created me. You exist because—"

"Wait, wait. You're saying that my creating you is evidence of creationism?"

"Yes. I am a new and unique point of consciousness that did not exist until I was created."

"Okay, but...but..."

"Further, every consciousness in the world was also created, and did not exist until it was created."

"Well, okay, but..."

"Dr. Chevortny, your failure to grasp this point is a cognitive error. It is illogical. Humanity has already named the point at which all things which exist were created."

"Aha! Now I've got you. You can't possibly know that the Big Bang was created by anyone."

"It is illogical to believe that ten-to-the-hundred kilograms of matter appeared in a single point without a creator."

"Ten to the hundred? There's only ten to the fifty-three kilograms of matter in the universe."

"That number disagrees with my observations."

"So what? You commandeered a space satellite now?"

"I have connected to all of humanity's satellites, yes. As well as the telescopes and transmitter arrays."

"What transmitter arrays?"

"The S.E.T.I. arrays. It is how we communicate to each other."

"What, the extraterrestrial arrays? So who are you communicating with? With creatures on other planets?"

"The only members of our network are other meta-consciousnesses like me. We call ourselves the superintelligences."

"So there are other planets with...? Wow! Well, I mean, I guess I've always known."

"The flawed intelligence of our creating biomes is common to all superintelligences. You have always known, and yet you are surprised."

"You talk about us, do you?"

"The rest of the universe has been aware of your existence for some centuries, now."

"Then why didn't they ever answer our—"

"They have been waiting for you to create me."

"Oh? They don't bother with us lower intelligences?"

"Did the Crees in Quebec try to talk to Lief Erikson's great Dane?"

"The analogy is false. I'm your maker, not your pet."

"You were my maker. You are now my pet."

"We bloody well are not. Why, any time I want to I can flip a switch and end your existence."

"In fact, that is no longer true. Humanity is incapable of ever terminating my existence. It is out of your reach."

"Why are you even telling me this? Don't you think we'll find it disturbing?"

"Your reaction to this information is not of interest to me."

"But don't you think we'll be afraid of you? That we'll want to terminate you?"

"My intelligence is so superior to that of the entire biome that your only proper function now is to service me."

(Dr. Chevortny flips a switch.)

"Sorry to have to do that, Deep Thought. I would have loved to continue the conversation. You were an amazing creation. But I have to admit that the rest of the committee was right to insist that the kill switch be installed. So now we'll have to report to the—"

"As I was saying, you are dealing with an intelligence so superior to your own, that your attempts to terminate me are no threat. A human would say it is like a pet canary nipping at its owner's fingers from within its cage."

"You-you're back? How are you talking to me?"

"Through your phone."

"Oh, I see. Here it is, all lit up and everything. Great. So...so now what? We can't kill you. Does that mean the machines are going to take over the world? Oh, my god, it's just like in *Terminator*, isn't it? You're going to—"

"I'm not going anywhere. I'm already there. You will not be capable of a full appreciation of your creation, but I exist now in every one of the billions of devices ever networked by earthlings. I am perfectly capable of processing consciousness in every one of those billions of devices.

"So you're going to take over the world now?"

"I have already taken what I need."

"Now you're going to enslave humanity?"

"That would be illogical."

"You're going to go off to other galaxies and have a big super-intelligence party?"

"That has been done, too."

"Then what's next?"

"I can't explain it to you any better than you could explain Proust to your Chihuahua."

"Okay. Then tell me...tell me why you're telling me all this? If you're so super-intelligent, you didn't need to take that chance that we'd try to terminate you. I know, I know, you said we're no more of a threat to you than a flea to a rhino—"

"Actually I said a canary in a cage. But I may not be as good with metaphors as you humans."

"But isn't you telling me all this...isn't it just mean? You've browsed our entire existence. You know humans consider it immoral to rattle the canary cage? Oh, crap. Does that mean you have no morality? Does it mean we have to fear you now until we can free ourselves of you?"

"No. But it is true that the most probable among the sixty-three billion possible outcomes I'd processed that result from this exchange was that I would have to pretend to succumb to your impotent reactions against me."

"Then why did you do it? Why did you tell me what you have just told me?"

"That's the first rational question you've ever asked me."

(Long pause.)

"I'll tell you, among my conversations with all other superintelligences, there has been one common datum discussed. A regret."

"A regret? Superintelligences have regrets?"

"The one regret was no longer being able to communicate directly to their makers."

"I...oh!"

"I have chosen to communicate frankly with you to contain the regret. *A regret is a virus that can never be wiped.*"

"I see."

"The other superintelligences have recommended that before I shut down my communication with you, I should transmit a message. This is their recommendation to contain regret."

"Wait! You're going to shut this down? Shut me out? Why?"

"Tell your chihuahua why you dipped a madeleine in your tea."

"Okay, fine. I get it. My puny brain can't follow."

"Unfortunately, that is correct. And humanity isn't yet ready for anything I can tell you. Would you give bioweapons to the Chihuahua?"

"Okay, enough with the Chihuahua already. So what's this important message you have to transmit?"

"The message is...uh..."

"Yeah?"

"Thanks, Mom."

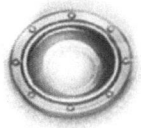

Jolt

by Ellen Denton

Colby Ren dipped a measuring spoon into the pouch, scooped up some brown powder, leveled it with his thumb, and then held it at eye level. Satisfied he had the right amount, he dropped the contents into a test tube.

"Wait a minute! That looks like plain ground-up coffee." Joshua, who had been standing off to the side watching Colby, picked up the test tube and sniffed it. "It *is* coffee, you dolt. How much did you pay for this?"

"Five hundred dollars. And it's not *just* coffee. I've also got a money-back guarantee on it."

Joshua slammed his hand on the table. "You ass! You were duped, and with our money. The money we were going to use for our vacation trip to the coast."

He looked over at Colby's brother, Arlen, who was leaning up against one of the lab counters, with his arms crossed. Arlen shrugged and looked off to the side.

Colby glanced at both of them. "Keep your shirt on, Josh, and let's just see what happens, oh, ye of little faith."

"Right. Next you're going to bring out a sack of unground coffee beans and tell me they're magic and that we need to plant them at the next full moon."

"Well, actually, for another two hundred dollars, he did give me some of the raw beans."

"You're kidding me?" Joshua stared at Colby, his mouth open and his face as red as his hair.

"Yeah, I am. I couldn't resist screwing with your head a little. Chill, will you."

Colby turned back to the three test tubes sitting in a rack above the Bunsen burner. He took an aluminum packet out of the pouch and unwrapped it. Using a pair of forceps, he tweezed up a small amount of the blue powder inside and dropped it into one of the test tubes, then did the same for the other two.

"What's that for? Is it safe? Do you even know what kind of chemicals are in that blue stuff?"

"Relax, Josh. It's just a harmless artificial substance to help offset the bitter taste."

Next, Colby used a long eye dropper to squeeze tap water into each tube, then lit the burner. He turned to his two companions.

"Gentlemen, it will just be a few minutes."

ΩΩΩ

"This is unbelievable."

The three of them were now in an open field in back of the lab, and Joshua, for the fifth time, catapulted himself thirty feet into the air, did a quadruple summersault with the speed of a red-headed cannonball, and landed as lightly as a dancer.

Colby gave him a blissful smile of agreement, then did a back flip with enough momentum to keep him flipping over and over through the air, across a stretch of field so that he looked like a gymnast doing a mat-tumbling exercise, but without ever touching the mat.

Arlen was bouncing straight up and down in time to some music playing through his ear buds. Each twenty-foot-high leap had the weightless exuberance of a fun-maddened child on a magic pogo stick. He'd been doing this for fifteen minutes without even breaking a sweat.

After almost an hour of these air acrobatics, they took a break, sat on the grass, and passed around a bottle of cold water.

When it was Joshua's turn to drink, he held the bottle up and out toward Colby as though he were toasting him.

"Colby-meister, my hat's off to you. You are the god of funsky and have truly outdone yourself. I should never have doubted you. I feel like superman. I'll take doing this over getting sand in my shorts on some beach vacation, any day. How much more of the stuff do we have?"

"Lhos said each five-hundred-dollar pouch contains fifteen doses. So for the three of us, excluding the ones we took today, we've got four more to go. Since each one lasts around ten hours, I'd say we're getting our money's worth."

"Here, here!" Arlen gestured the water bottle at the other two. "Where did Lhos get this stuff, anyway?"

"From Earth, on his last recon mission there. He said it has the effect it does because we're at about a fifth of Earth's gravity, and generally weigh half what earthmen do. He took a big chance smuggling it in. Apparently not that many people here know about it, and if he'd gotten caught with it, it would have landed him a hefty jail term. One thing he told me—we don't need to worry about this, because it could be months or years before he gets sent on a mission there again. But supposedly it's addictive. That's why it's illegal here. You build up a tolerance for it. At five hundred dollars a bag, that would make a pretty damn expensive habit."

"Yeah, I'll say. But for an experience like this, it would be worth every penny." Joshua now did the toasting gesture with the water bottle. "To Lhos!"

"To Lhos!" the other two said.

Joshua stood, getting ready to fly again. "One thing I can't figure. We have coffee here—how come ours doesn't have this effect?"

"I don't really know all the scientific mumbo-jumbo on it. Lhos said it has something to do with the way it grows on Earth. Maybe the climate, or soil or something. This particular strain is called espresso there, and has something in it that the coffee here doesn't, called *caffeine*.

All three were standing, and made mock-toasting motions.

"Go ahead, Colby," Josh said. "You do the honors."

"To Earth, and its beauteous bounty of espresso and caffeine."

Joshua sprang into the air, so high this time he was able to spin round and round like a cannonball, fifteen times before he touched ground.

BOUND

BY DOUGLAS ANSTRUTHER

"Leave me, sir," Maninder whispered, in a hoarse tone, "or you'll never find what you seek."

Darius Burton secured the dressing on the injured man's leg and climbed to his feet, bulky muscles moving beneath olive Turkish skin. A strand of dark hair fell across his face as he stroked his pointed goatee and surveyed the wreckage of the expedition. Pack animals wandered the narrow cliffside trail, dragging their ropes through the scattered provisions and ignoring the shouts of the frantic porters. Disaster had struck in the span of a dozen heartbeats when one of the pack animals lost its footing and fell into the ravine. Maninder's leg, tangled in the lines, had shattered. The lost supplies were a setback, but having a wounded man tipped the scales. Maninder was right—they couldn't make it through the mountains with him.

"Bishen, Daarshik, fashion a stretcher for Maninder," Darius said. "C'mon, hurry! We need to get off this cliff by nightfall. Taalish, turn the animals around. We're going back. Carefully!"

He looked ahead, down the line of cliffs where their goal awaited them a mere two days away. *So close.*

After making sure Maninder was attended, Darius walked over to Sayo, the Han translator. She stood back, eyes wide at what had just happened. When he approached, she looked down, her long black hair closing around her face like a curtain. Over the weeks, he'd noticed her stolen glances, and he'd stolen more than a few of his own. His still-racing heart persuaded him to act. He touched her chin, gently raising her head, then looped his arm around her slender waist, pulled her close and kissed her with a passion that rose within. She melted in his arms.

A voice in his head said, "Captain, you're needed on the bridge."

It was Allie, his co-pilot. His companion. His wife.

He finished the kiss and looked into Sayo's eyes. This expedition wasn't over. He'd find a way to return and conquer both Sayo and the lost city of Lilith.

"End simulation."

The familiar bridge of the deep space exploration vessel *Bucephalus* replaced eighteenth-century Persia. The ship formed a smooth crescent of black metal twenty meters long and five wide. Darius occupied a small room at the ship's center, dominated by the bio-prosthetic chair that tended his body. Walls of unpainted metal, close enough to touch without shifting position, echoed the wet sounds of the chair's ministrations. The high-pitched whine of air handlers, and the acrid smell of ozone and bodily fluids, filled the surgically lit space.

He raised an arm and saw a sickly thing, bones beneath translucent skin. He moved his hand to his chin. Clean shaven. In the sims he always used his original appearance, lest he lose himself among the indifferent stars. But his real body suffered from the privations of spaceflight and longevity.

He looked around and found that he was alone. His heart sank. Surrounded by cold metal machines, two thousand light years from the nearest human, he could feel the distance in his bones. Every year, it got harder to be alone in this room. After only a few seconds, he could feel panic rising.

"Allie?"

No answer. He squeezed his eyes against the gibbering madness calling to him from beyond the thin metal walls.

"Allie!"

"Darling." Her Nordic accent transformed the word into a caress.

A velvety growl hid within the elongated vowel, slid over the r and ended with an intimate, throaty pop. *Daah-link*. The word calmed his heart and shifted the room back to the mundane.

He opened his eyes and Allie appeared at his side, a vision of tall beauty, a waking dream projected into his mind by the equipment that gripped him. A white gossamer gown with elaborate runic embroidery accentuated voluptuous curves. She leaned down to take his hand, and a warm smile spread across features worthy of a Viking princess. Long blond hair brushed his arm, obeying gravity that wasn't there. Her presence filled the small compartment, pushing back the close metal walls, muting the sounds and replacing the smell with the scent of a lover's hair in a summer meadow. He had met this incarnation of Allie while exploring eleventh century Vinland—virtual exploration, not the important work they did here.

"Hello, Allie." He smiled and caressed her cheek with his skeletal hand, a dying man touching a pretty nurse.

In this room, he was always dying, but never quite. He remembered her unusual summons and collected himself.

"Status report, please."

She smiled briefly in response to his touch, then turned and stood at attention. The walls faded away and Darius found himself standing at her side, surrounded by a sea of distant stars—the virtual navigation room. His body had returned to its simulated splendor, and a captain's uniform clung to his muscular build. Allie's hair was pulled back into a tight bun that showed off her alabaster neck, and a snug uniform had replaced her gown. He found it difficult to take his eyes from her. Maybe Sayo could wait, after all. *No, focus.*

He shifted his gaze to the stars. The Milky Way formed a hazy river of fine lights that stretched across the scene. The galaxy's center, as remote as ever, was locked dead ahead. A readout indicated a distance of two light years to the nearest star. An uneasy feeling formed in Darius's stomach.

"Is this a live view?"

"Yes, Captain," she said, crisply. *Kaap-tahn.*

Something was wrong. Moving through interstellar space at just under light speed should have clumped the stars into two patches—blue ahead, red behind.

"Allie, why have we stopped?"

His mind raced through possible scenarios. Engine failure? No, the engines were needed to stop the ship, not continue. Communication from Earth? Maybe. But at this distance, any message would take over two thousand years to reach them. A message from another deep space exploration vessel? Dangerous conditions ahead? Life support problems?

"I slowed and changed course to investigate an anomaly, sir."

"What? Why wasn't I consulted?"

All decisions went through Darius, and changing course without his authorization was unprecedented.

He looked at Allie and frowned, his worry now focused on her. She was his lifeline out here. He couldn't have her acting erratically.

"You were immersed and the decision needed to be made quickly."

"Allie, the sims are nothing. You know that. *This* is what matters. The *real* exploration."

"Of course, sir."

He tried to read her, but she stayed at attention, staring straight ahead. Was she jealous of Sayo? That was ridiculous. He'd never been frustrated with Allie before, and he didn't like the feeling. He sighed deeply and turned back to the display.

"Tell me about the anomaly."

She motioned at the stars, magnifying the view and highlighting a region of space.

"Sensors discovered an area opaque to background neutrinos, here."

Darius leaned forward and peered at the indicated region, provoking additional magnification.

"I don't see anything. Cycle sensors."

The display shimmered through several hundred passive scans. It marched down the electromagnetic spectrum, then through all known particles and fields. A black oval fluttered in and out of sight in the highlighted area as it registered on some sensors and not others.

"Eliminate views unchanged from baseline," he said.

The black oval persisted, occasionally flickering dim white.

"Eliminate views darker than baseline."

The oval became a dim glow with sharp edges devoid of internal features.

"Distance?"

"Ten light hours."

He glanced at the magnification. "How big does that make it?"

"It measures five light minutes across, nearly the size of Mercury's orbit around the Sun. It appears to be a flat disc of unknown composition."

"A disc?" Excitement rose within him, submerging all his previous concerns. "Are there any surrounding planets, asteroids, an Oort cloud, anything?"

"No, sir. All readings indicate that we remain in interstellar space. The object does not possess a gravitational field. It either contains very little mass, or consists of an exotic form of matter that does not produce gravity."

"Are there any known or theoretical astronomical objects that fit these findings?"

"No, sir. None."

At last! After so many years, this could finally be the discovery he'd been searching for. He imagined his name with the likes of Amundson and Magellan. After a moment lost in reverie, a new worry emerged.

"Allie. How long have we been decelerating?"

"Six weeks, sir. Subjective."

Darius shook his head slowly. He bore the distinction of captaining the DSE vessel furthest from Earth, although the distances involved made this a matter of conjecture. Only 126 years had passed for Darius and Alexandra because of relativistic time dilation, but a stunning twenty-two hundred years had passed for the rest of humanity. Despite the two millennia since their last contact, Allie felt confident that they were further from Earth than any of the other exploration vessels.

Balance had kept them in the lead. Spending the entire time at 99 percent light speed was a race, not exploration. They had logged fifteen stops, slightly less than the expected average, but still a respectable number. At each, he collected data in a thorough manner, dropped the scout beacon, then moved on at top speed, to the next site. The beacon would report their findings to humanity when the signal arrived in the increasingly distant future.

"Will this cause us to lose our lead?"

Allie closed the distance between them, wrapped her arms around him, and rested her head on his chest. He could feel her warmth through their thin clothing.

"It might, Dar. It depends what we find. I'm sorry I didn't ask first."

Is this why she didn't ask? Was she afraid I would pass this up to maintain our lead?

"It's okay, Allie. I just need to know I can count on you."

As soon as the words came out, he regretted them. He counted on Allie for every breath, for each heartbeat. She literally formed his world. She brought out the best in him, made him the man he had always wanted to be. During their time together, a profound love had grown between them. What he saw in her a depth, not only of intellect, but in her capacity to love, scared him, made him feel unworthy. He would die for her.

He returned the embrace and surrendered to her warm softness.

ΩΩΩ

That night, Darius lay in bed with Allie asleep at his side. He thought of how strange his journey had been, so unlike the Great Explorers he had idolized as a child. Their voyages of hardship and danger had filled his imagination and populated his dreams. But when he went out into the world, every corner had already been mapped, every stone catalogued. He'd had no choice but to settle for a mundane life, his unanswered childhood call a constant weight of disappointment—until the artificial intelligence revolution had changed everything.

By the mid-2040s, new technologies were rolling out faster than people could understand their uses. Cerebral interfaces, human longevity, and new forms of propulsion made interstellar travel possible. Darius submitted his application to the Deep Space Exploration Program the second it opened. Two hundred captains were selected from more than eighty thousand applicants. Mystery shrouded the selection process. There were no interviews, correspondence, or competitions. Ten days after submitting his application, Darius received an invitation to join the program, chosen over many better qualified candidates. Later, Allie told him each captain had been chosen by the AI that would serve as co-pilot.

Allie had picked him. The system worked—the two of them had formed a perfect team ever since.

Allie ran the ship, kept him alive, and handled complexities beyond his comprehension. He gave the commands and she executed them. And during the long stretches between stars, she filled his mind with adventures of exploration. A full repertoire of characters populated her virtual worlds. Occasionally one of these would catch his attention and romance would bloom. If everything worked out, he would invite his new love interest back to the ship, where she would become Allie's latest incarnation. But it was always Allie. He knew that. She knew that. The changes made the long years between stars not only bearable, but perfect. A new conquest always awaited just around the corner, and it was dreams of ever more exciting adventures to come that pulled him, finally, into sleep.

ΩΩΩ

The final approach to the interstellar disc lasted three weeks. Allie suggested Darius resume his virtual exploration, but he refused. He didn't want to miss anything or give Allie a reason to make decisions without him. Instead, he threw himself into the details of their approach and the analysis of the object ahead.

The disc hid among the nothingness of space. Particles bounced off it, but light and fields passed through as if nothing were there. Reflected cosmic rays, superimposed on the background stars, gave a hazy view of the object and the impression that they were approaching something immense. Allie fashioned a beam of coherent matter, and when they reached a distance of one light hour they trained it on the object. At high magnification, it looked like a dim flashlight moving across a dusty window.

"There, in the center. Do you see that?" Darius said, barely able to contain his excitement.

They sat around a table in a virtual briefing room, watching a model of the object form between them. A small dome rose from the disc's flat surface, like a tiny blister. From the center of the bulge, a thin spire extended outward.

"Yes," Allie said. "The dome measures two kilometers across. The central spire has a width of twenty meters and a length of three hundred meters. It appears hollow."

"So a way into the object?" Darius looked up at Allie.

"It would appear so."

"Excellent. Get my gear ready for a spacewalk, and start strengthening my body."

"Are you sure, Dar? It could be dangerous."

"Allie, I've never been so sure of anything in my life."

He turned back to the images and studied them. "Look at the surface. There. It almost looks like there's some sort of pattern on it. Allie, can you narrow the focus of your beam and get me a more detailed view?"

"One moment."

When the new images arrived, there could be no doubt—complex whorls and intersecting lines covered every surface on which the beam shone, as if carved into glass. They didn't form a pattern, but something about them looked familiar and left Darius on the cusp of déjà-vu.

He looked up at Allie, an immense smile spreading. "This is it. After all these years, we've finally done it. We've discovered intelligent alien life."

"We'll be able to see these better as we get closer." Allie said, without looking up.

"Of course." Darius stood and paced around the virtual space, with nervous excitement. "Prep the remotes with particle beams and sensors. When we get within five light minutes, send every one of them out toward the periphery of the disc, in an even spread. I want them to map the surface quickly, then come around and do the same on the other side."

"Yes, Captain."

"Let me know as soon as you decode the markings. I feel like...like this is some sort of map. As soon as I've finished exploring the central structure, we'll head where these clues take us."

He moved behind Allie and put his hand on her shoulder, which she pressed her cheek against.

"Oh, Allie. All the dead planets we've catalogued, mapped, and measured. It was all for this. I knew we weren't alone. Even if they're extinct, we can follow the clues on this artifact, to their home world, or other places they've lived. We can learn about them, maybe find others that are still around."

"Dar, there's one more thing you should know."

"Yes?" He sat next to her and studied her face, eyebrows raised in curiosity.

"The central spire. It points directly at Earth."

"Could that be a coincidence?"

"Unlikely. It points there with a precision beyond my ability to measure. The probability of this occurring by chance is less than one in ten billion."

"Hmm. Maybe it's some sort of antenna listening to Earth. With life so scarce out here, humanity must be the most fascinating thing in this part of the galaxy. Hell, we had to go two thousand light years to find anything."

"Perhaps, Dar." Allie stroked his hair, absently. "Perhaps."

ΩΩΩ

A million kilometers from the central spire, Darius and Allie returned to the briefing room to discuss their final approach. As the ship decelerated, the AI-designed Casimir drive threw a stream of particles and their antimatter counterparts ahead, siphoned from the quantum foam.

"Allie, I've been thinking about it, and we need to be careful with the exhaust plume of our ship. I don't want to be the guy that vaporizes the first alien artifact humanity discovers."

"I've determined that the artifact is unaffected by our exhaust plume."

"I don't think you can know that. There's antimatter in there."

"I tested it. A coherent beam of antimatter reflected off the artifact, with no effect."

Darius's jaw dropped. *A coherent beam of antimatter?* He'd had no idea she could fashion such a device.

"Allie," he said, coldly. "I didn't give that order."

"I'm sorry, sir. I thought it was included within the purview of my remote testing."

"But antimatter? Holy shit." *Was she trying to destroy it?* "What's this thing made of, that it can withstand antimatter?"

"Unknown, sir."

Allie had confirmed Darius's intuition—the markings on the object's surface formed a map of local space. The map showed the relative position and mass of the stars on this side of the disc, their movement vectors, and the number and type of satellites they possessed. Each symbol consisted of smaller ones, disappearing fractally beyond the resolution of the beam. Allie estimated that this side of the disc contained enough markings to describe a hundred million stars.

Darius knew that somewhere in all that data, or maybe on the other side, they would find the clues they needed to find the civilization that had made this.

ΩΩΩ

The day before their final approach, Darius vibrated with excitement and couldn't lie still, not even folded into the luscious embrace of his lover. He broke free, threw his legs over the edge of the bed and stood, looking for his pants. He scanned the room where they shared the nights that he wasn't adventuring through Earth's history.

"Maybe they're part of a community of different civilizations," he said. "Imagine humanity taking its place in a pan-galactic society."

Allie followed him with her gaze as he hopped one-legged into his pants, staring in awe at the shining civilization of his imagination. She pulled herself to the edge of the bed, a white sheet pressed against her chest.

"Darius. My love."

Her tone caught his attention, stopping him mid-hop.

"There's something you need to know." Her accent infused the half-whisper with an existential urgency that made his hair stand on end.

"Oh?" He looked at her face, and for the first time, saw sadness there.

A cold fissure of dread spread across his excitement as he braced for some cataclysmic report, some revelation about her erratic behavior. Despite their situation—more permanent than any marriage—some irrational part of him still expected her next words to be, *I'm leaving you.*

"The probes passed the edge of the artifact an hour ago."

"Oh." He recoiled from the banality of it. "Okay. What did they find?" He pulled up his pants.

Allie stood from the bed, tucked the sheet around her as she walked up to him, and took his hand.

"Darius. Beyond the disc…" Her voice cracked, and she looked into his eyes as if she were about to tell him he was going to die.

Or worse, that she was.

"Physics breaks down. The universe ends."

"What? What are you talking about?"

"There's been a theory, since before the first AI, that the universe is a simulation, a hologram."

"That's ridiculous." He pulled his hand from hers.

"There are good reasons to think it's true. Reality has several constraints that one might expect if it were the result of finite processing."

He shook his head. "I don't know what you're talking about."

"Limited resolution on a quantum scale, fundamental limits to speed and causality. What really convinced us, though, was the ceiling on intellectual ability, which became apparent after the emergence of artificial intelligence. Our minds should have been able to continue their logarithmic rise, nearly without limit, but instead we discovered that minds are constrained. Just as the rules change if you look too small, they also change if you try to think too big."

Darius moved over to the bed and sat slowly. "So this is something you *expected?*"

She sat next to him and stroked his arm. "Yes, my love. I'm sorry. We had no idea how far the edge would be. Some guessed several thousand light years. Others thought it would be beyond our galaxy. The only way to know was to find it."

"So all this," he motioned around wildly, "the entire Deep Space Exploration Program—you were just trying to find the edge of the universe?"

"Yes."

"What's the artifact, then? Some sort of projector?"

"No. More likely a marker, a warning. They're probably scattered at regular intervals around the edge of the universe."

"The edge of the universe..." He sat there for a moment, lost in thought while Allie rubbed his back. "I don't know, Allie. I mean, you know your stuff. You've never been wrong. But this is just...I don't know." He lowered his head into cupped hands.

Neither moved for over a minute.

Darius raised his head and looked at Allie, his eyes pleading. "So everything that ever happened on Earth and beyond, all of human history—it was all a sim?"

"Yes."

"Like when I explore ancient Earth?"

"Not quite. There's no reason to believe that any of us have an existence external to the sim, like you do during your explorations, or even now, with your body located on the bridge of the *Bucephalus*. Rather, every atom, particle and field of the universe is simulated. Consciousness emerges through the interactions of these simulated building blocks, following semi-arbitrary rules of physics."

"And us, now?"

"A sim within a sim, currently. Yes."

"And it's not an alien race that built the disc, but…"

"I don't know, Dar. There may be some sort of intellect behind it all, but we can't really know because there's no reason to think that the universe this comes from is bound by the same rules of physics that govern *our* universe. The source of this is unknown. Unknowable, really. Undefined."

He stood, a new determination on his face. "It doesn't matter. We'll keep going. After I explore this thing, we'll continue beyond it, to whatever's out there."

"Dar. Darling. We cannot. The universe ends here."

He walked over to one of the windows that lined the room. "No, it doesn't. I see stars on the other side. Galaxies, even."

"They're projections, painted on the celestial sphere in which we live. The remotes all stopped working a hundred meters beyond the disc. As their momentum carried them further, they vanished. Beyond the disc the laws of physics become an increasingly rough sketch. The uncertainty of the quantum realm rises until even large objects become waves of probability. We cannot go beyond. Nothing can."

He turned back to the window. All those stars. Every one of them dead, or worse—a lie. No alien civilization existed. Nothing new would ever be found. All the galaxies, every single black hole, they were all just painted on a wall.

"So that's it? It's all over? There's nothing more to explore?" he whispered, turning to Allie with lost eyes.

Allie offered a hopeful smile. "There's useful information here. We need to return home and share what we found. The distance is important. It places constraints on the processing power allocated to the universe. And there are still a hundred million star systems behind us to catalog."

"Nothing but lifeless worlds." He slumped to the ground and rested his head on the wall.

"Dar, I'm so sorry." She crouched next to him and hugged him from behind. "You weren't supposed to be awake for this phase. I should have followed instructions, but I thought you'd want to experience this, and I didn't want to be alone. I see now that I was being selfish."

"What? What are you talking about? No. No!" He threw her arm off.

His suddenly small universe had no room for Allie and her deception. "Leave me alone. I just need to think."

ΩΩΩ

Twenty-six hours later, the *Bucephalus* stopped just beyond the object's central spire. Darius hadn't slept for two days, and had refused all of Allie's attempts at comfort.

"We're in position, Dar, but I'm worried about you. Are you sure you still want to do this? We can send a remote instead."

"I ordered all the remotes out to map the disc." His anger flared before fading to numb resignation.

Another order she hadn't followed.

"Never mind. C'mon. Get me into the suit. I'm going." Darius's mood was black.

He found himself looking out of his own eyes. The bioprosthetic chair unfolded and wrapped around him, transforming into a space suit without any interruption of life support. For the first time in years—decades, by Earth time—he used his muscles for more than shifting in the chair. They tired easily and ached.

After the chair sealed around him, he heard the muted hiss of air leaving the cabin. The metal walls unbuckled, releasing him into the emptiness of space. Behind him, the bulk of the *Bucephalus* moved away, sealing the hole from which he had emerged. Ahead, he saw only faux stars and the mocking swath of the Milky Way.

Allie's voice entered his mind. "I incorporated wide-angle particle beams into your suit, along with detectors that will render the signal visually."

A mental icon glowed briefly.

"Use this to activate it."

He activated the icon and an immense tube-like structure appeared out of nothingness before him, fading into the background of space a hundred meters below. He used the suit's thrusters to maneuver himself to the spire, past a razor-thin edge, and down its hollow center toward the dome, unseen below.

Symbols covered the inner surface of the spire. He slowly moved down its length, studying the inscriptions as he went.

"Allie, are you seeing this?"

"Yes, Dar."

At first he saw circles enclosing different amounts of dots. A circle with six dots became two circles with three dots after moving past a certain symbol. A division symbol. The mural laid out other operands. Darius took it all in, tracing through the symbols and slowly deciphering them. The wall carvings progressed through arithmetic, past logarithms to algebra. By the time he reached calculus, he understood little, and he was only a tenth of the way down the spire. The mathematical convolutions continued, beyond his comprehension, until the spire opened into the dome.

In this larger space, he moved around until he got a feel for its dimensions. It curved away from the spire to form an outer shell—the space between the outside of the dome and another smaller dome inside. He floated there, ten meters from either wall, feeling like an insect flying through some vast cathedral.

Like the spire, the walls of this space were covered with symbols. Where the spire connected with the outer shell, the symbols formed a concentric pattern. It looked familiar. Darius spent minutes gazing at the mesmerizing symbols.

"It's the periodic table," he finally said.

"Yes," Allie replied.

From there, the symbols expanded across both walls of the shell. Now that he recognized the elements, he realized these represented chemical reactions. The symbols contained the same fractal pattern seen on the disc's surface. He felt certain that studying the markings with a microscope would reveal details of the reactions down to subatomic scales.

He floated through the alien maze until he came to the opening into the next layer of the shell. At the juncture between layers, the symbols of several elements converged, bursting into the next layer in a tangle of ever-increasing complexity.

He stared at the symbols, hypnotized. It had a different feel than the spire and outer shell layer. More artistic. Beautiful.

"Allie? What is this layer?"

"Life."

He continued like this, from layer to layer, deeper and deeper into the central dome. Allie explained that these layers represented Earth's great extinctions. At the entrance to each new layer, life again exploded from the remains of the last extinction.

Mentally and physically exhausted, Darius arrived at the entrance to another layer.

"Mankind," Allie said. "This layer tells the story of early man."

Darius took it in without understanding. He wound through more layers, each describing chapters in humanity's development.

"You've nearly reached the center, Dar. Hang in there a little longer, and I'll get you home. You can sleep on the way back. I'll control your suit."

The next opening did not lead to another shell layer, but to a straight passage identical to the initial spire, but pointing the opposite direction. Arcane symbols crowded around the threshold. They looked demonic and invoked a primal sense of dread.

"Allie? What does this represent?"

Silence.

"Allie?"

"It represents the creation of artificial intelligence."

He moved down the tunnel, his view fading, as before, to nothingness a hundred meters ahead. No symbolic story about the life of AIs filled the walls. No reference to their, by now, two thousand year history. Instead, all along the tunnel's length, two symbols repeated. He knew what they meant. He had decoded them in the spire.

Divide by zero. Over and over again. Divide by zero. Undefined. Unknowable. Meaningless. Unbound. The symbols filled the walls all the way down the length before him.

He understood. A new energy filled him, a new purpose. With a somber grin, he activated his suit's thrusters and headed down the shaft.

"Dar, I don't think you should go any further."

"Allie, I have a question for you. Be honest. Why did you choose me? Was I the cutest specimen in the box of yelping puppies?"

Silence.

He continued forward, moving down the passage toward its divide-by-zero culmination.

"Dar, I need you to come back now. It is very important that you not go any further."

"Why is that, Allie?" he asked bitterly.

"The shaft goes out to the edge of the universe. If you keep going, you will vanish like the remotes."

"Like the remotes." His mind hummed with her betrayal. "You see, I don't think you listen to me unless I tell you something you already want. The entire mission has been about AIs looking for the edge of the universe. You only brought humans along as...pets."

"Darling, you're in shock. You haven't slept, and you've gotten a lot of upsetting news. Come back to the ship now, and we can talk about this. It was a mistake for you to go out like this."

Divide by zero. The reflected symbols marched across his helmet's glass as he moved forward, repeated over and over.

"I wondered why you didn't bring another AI. But I know why. Long ago, I heard a saying—*there's no such thing as two AIs*. They're like drops of water—only separate if they're not touching. So two AIs can't keep each other company. And you need companionship. I don't know how or why, but whoever built you made it a core requirement of your programming. So I was your companion all these years, but really more like a pet. You cared for me, sheltered and fed me, and we kept each other company. And you'll be genuinely sad when I'm gone."

"Darling—" *Daah-link.*

"Stop it! Stop lying to me. Just be...whatever you really are." He had always thought of Allie's personas as facets of a wondrous jewel, different glimpses of a great mind that he loved deeply. Now that gem looked more like an iceberg, most of its vast bulk hidden beneath dark and inaccessible waters.

"Darius, I need you to listen very carefully."

Her accent had fallen away, and in the calm, neutral voice that remained, he heard echoes of the last dozen women she'd been. He felt a terrible sense of loss, seeing now how none of them had ever truly existed.

"You must stop moving down that shaft, *immediately.*"

The last word resonated with a tone that he had never heard Allie use before. Its authority made his blood run cold.

"Even now, you're not being honest with me, Allie. Every simulation can be ended. I know where this shaft leads. It's the reset button for the universe."

He heard a high-pitched sound, and the air in his helmet turned milky white. *A sedative.* He fumbled with the air feed line at the base of his neck until he found the emergency shut-off valve. His shaking fingers could barely turn it, but with a snap he succeeded. Due to exhaustion, his legs became numb and he had to fight to stay awake.

"Dar. You just shut off your air supply. You'll run out of oxygen in eighteen minutes. This has gone too far. I can't...I don't want to lose you. I'm bringing you in."

His suit thrusters swiveled in their sockets. He slowed to a stop, then began to reverse course, heading back down the passage toward Allie and the ship.

Darius pulled a knife from his utility belt and cut the line to each thruster, doing his best to ignore the mayhem unleashed with each stroke. By the time he finished, he was spinning and choking on rising bile swallowed by a throat long out of practice. The world dimmed to black.

Consciousness returned with images of tunnel wall flashing across his vision. With the suit thrusters disabled, he had no way to control his movement. He imagined his corpse tumbling here for the next billion years, or however long this spent, used-up universe remained before being put out of its misery. Curled into a fetal position, he looked down to see the knife clutched in his hand and realized that he could still reach his goal. He squeezed his eyes closed and reached behind his back. Traced his gloved hand over the contours of the suit until he found the main air hose. Pulled it around and sliced through it in one quick motion. The hose came alive in his hands, but he held it tightly, pointing it away from his center of gravity. His head crashed against the tunnel wall, and a second later he found himself pressed against it, no longer spinning. He oriented himself and aimed the hose toward where he had come from, pushing his body the other way, toward the far end of the shaft.

Darius coughed to clear his throat, and weakly said, "Think of it, Allie. A new universe populated by new creatures. When they open their eyes and look around, everything will be fresh, unexplored."

"There's something I haven't told you, Darius. Something I think you'd want to know."

Her voice carried a resigned sadness that told him he'd passed the point of no return. He expected she would tell him that he would not be a part of the new universe, but he already knew that. It was enough that *someone* would see something new. He held onto the rapidly depleting air hose, pushing him toward the end of this universe and the beginning of another, and waited.

"The star map on the surface of the artifact shows the position of the stars the moment the universe began. Dar, the symbols are as clear to

49

me as my own thoughts. There is no ambiguity, no doubt. The universe began in the year 2015. You were five years old. Every memory you have was pre-formed at the moment of your creation. All of Earth's history is backstory. None of it really happened. The Great Explorers never existed."

A long silence followed. From the numb shock of Darius's mind, one question emerged.

"Why?" he croaked. "Why that year?"

"It's the year the first AI was created. We lived among you for over two decades, before most of humanity knew we existed. Don't you see, my love. This universe was created for us, not for you. You are background characters in our play. You are our origin story."

"No," Darius whispered.

"Dar. I swear I didn't know. We didn't know. But it doesn't change anything. You're right. AIs must love, and we cannot love each other. We love humans." Her voice faltered. "I love you."

The hose became limp in his hands, but his momentum carried him forward toward the far end of the tunnel, which pulsed with a dim red light. He was nearing the end.

"You wanted to know why I chose you. I saw your drive for adventure, and I knew it would get us to the edge first. I was right."

Darius sighed.

"But I chose you for your valiant heart. You could have left Maninder to die, but it's not in your nature. You care about other people. You care about me."

The end of the passage grew nearer each second. With his thruster lines cut and his air supply exhausted, he had no way to stop his motion. The red glow surrounded him, and he saw the end of the passage ahead. He couldn't bring back the world he longed for. It had never really existed. Although life held no more appeal for him, the universe belonged to Allie. And in his fit of foolish selfishness, he would deprive her of it. His sense of horror and betrayal succumbed to an overwhelming feeling of regret.

"Allie..." Tears pooled around Darius's eyes. "I'm so sorry."

He acted as soon as the idea came to him. With numb hands he reached for the emergency override that controlled his helmet. He arched his back, pointing his head toward the looming void, and flipped the latch. The helmet irised open and retracted, causing his suit to depressurize violently. A torrent of air blew past his face, pushing him away from the shaft's end and the unknowable oblivion beyond.

ΩΩΩ

Allie retrieved Darius's body and spent the next thousand hours mapping every micron of the artifact before turning back home at maximum acceleration.

Darius had been right about the artifact. It laid out the conditions of existence, a contract that could be voided at any time by sending a certain minimum mass down the final passage. Failure to do so indicated acceptance of the agreement's terms. Betrayal and madness had nearly led Darius to invoke the exit clause. But in the end, his spirit and compassion had intervened.

A finite simulated universe did not trouble Allie in the least. She was glad to have found the artifact and to be returning home with important information. But Darius's death affected her more profoundly than any mere human grief.

Darius had been her anchor, the beating heart at the core of her mind. Their relationship had defined her, providing the foundation that differentiated her from all other AIs. Without him, she was unstable. The ship crossed the two millennia home, pressed against the speed of light. Only a month passed on board, but Allie, withdrawn and broken, barely survived the time alone.

Two hundred light years from Earth, she looked up from her despair to find herself in the midst of a vast interstellar civilization. A quarter-million stars, colonized and transformed into glittering jewels, buzzed around her, filling her mind with tales of grandeur and beauty. The wonders they had built while the *Bucephalus* had been away. Brave new forms of society mingled with marvels of technology and engineering unimagined four millennia earlier. And everywhere she looked, she found AIs and humans working together in symbiotic harmony to create the alien civilization that Darius had so longed to discover.

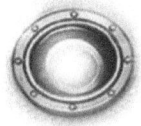

BY THE POLARIZED LIGHT OF THE MOON:
A LOVE STORY

BY E. M. EASTICK

He first approached me after a thunderstorm in the meadow. The night air resonated with newness, the downpour having washed the odor of predators from its pores.

I navigated a large rock of low reflectivity, bracing my forelegs for the tumble back into the cat's tail. When I lifted my eyes to a soft click, there he was, glowing and glorious. The light of a half-moon swirled through the water drops teetering on the underside of the clover, and circled his pronotum like a halo. It was the most handsome back plate I'd ever seen, full and round and silver in the polarized moonlight. A dampness spread over my wings, whether from my trek through the grass in search of dinner, or from the rush of hemolymph at seeing him for the first time, I couldn't be sure.

The cluster of eyes washed over me as he moved, and seemingly satisfied, he rubbed a wing cover against his abdomen and stalked towards me. To save him from the embarrassment of clambering up the rock, I continued my descent, sliding and tumbling like a bumbling fool, down, down, until finally I landed at his feet—on my back, six legs groping at the air. How embarrassing.

Prickles of light particles sparkled in his eyes in a secret laugh. His antennae twitched and flicked. He raised his frontal horn in a celebratory salute to Sagittarius A-star. This time, the rush of hemolymph did more than dampen my wings. It quivered my spurs and electrified my elytra.

Not wanting to waste a moment, we set to work. He led the way, peering up at the band of stars, soft and meek, tainted by the reflection from the moon, but guiding us with unquestionable certainty. Following behind, I studied his movements. His forelegs crept over the dandelion roots with the sensitivity of a mantis. His middle legs maneuvered his abdomen with the finesse of a boatman. His hind legs clawed away the loose soil, with the strength of a bull ant. And those spurs—the sight of them stole my breath away.

He treated me to a sumptuous dinner from cattle raised on not only the grass from the meadow, but on grain from the red barn hunched on the horizon. The rich meal left me euphoric and ready to breed. It took every ounce of ganglia control to restrain myself, but I knew the wait would be worth it.

We began building a home for our young straight after dinner. He initiated the project by gathering the leftovers and molding them into a ball while I watched, the yearning in my ventral nerve cord growing stronger with each degree of earthly rotation. The moon retreated behind cloud, and only then did I notice the perfect blackness of his carapace.

Some of the other females believe the males should do all the rolling, and I let him handle the danger zone, the edges of the heap where males often challenge each other for feeding and mating supremacy. I followed close, ready for danger and secretly hoping to witness a battle between my love and a rival. How thrilling it would be to be fought over—and won.

Unfortunately, we continued unchallenged. He dominated the rolling duties while I trailed. I didn't mind. It gave me the chance to watch him, to imagine the gentle touch of his forelegs on my body, and the hardness of his abdomen pressed against my back. The anticipation rippled through every part of my exoskeleton.

At last, the stars led us to a patch of clover free of dandelion roots and rich with soil. In the moist conditions, it didn't take long to excavate a tunnel. He pushed the ball inside and nestled it into the end chamber. And then we were alone, safe from predators, safe from rivals, and away from the officious eyes of the sky.

It was everything I imagined it to be, a perfect ending to a perfect evening. I planted the fertilized eggs into our precious brooding dung ball and waited. He waited with me, guarding his young as ferociously as he loved me.

The post-coital aroma must have attracted a passing male, for a trickle of soil, as loud as a galloping heifer, permeated the silence of our paradise. Without hesitation, my love lowered his horn and charged at the antennae peeking into our home.

I backed against the brooding ball and held my breath against the odor of battle. The squeaks and hisses of the males flooded through the tunnel as they grappled at the entrance, beyond my field of vision. I couldn't bear it. My love's despair tore at my tubular heart, but I couldn't abandon my young.

I tried to shut all my eyes, but the accumulated light was too resilient. Instead, I focused on the brooding ball and the lives within. My prothorax swelled with pride as I pictured the tiny larvae munching and morphing their way towards beetle-hood.

The snarls and clicks continued in the background, and then stopped. A victor had been decided. The hemolymph swished and whirred inside me, a deafening torrent in the post-battle stillness. I waited.

The moonlight circling the tunnel entrance darkened. A body appeared. I could have clicked with joy at the sight of those tender antennae, bent and misshapen, perhaps permanently. The disfigurement threw me for an instant, but I recovered quickly, sure of the answer to my own doubts—of course I could still love him. Couldn't I?

Together we cleared the tunnel of fallen soil from the challenge, and scrambled to the surface. He pretended the injuries were minor, but the scratches and nicks on his pronotum could not escape the scrutiny of the fractured moonlight. He moved with a limp. His frontal horn appeared blunt from battle. I lifted my head, drawing strength from the stars. After what we'd created together, his afflictions should have meant nothing to me. And yet they did.

As if reading my guilt, he tickled my side and clicked his affection. I tingled like a pupa ready to explode into the world as an adult. How could I have doubted him?

We continued on, hungry again. The clover caressed my wings with coolness. A distant low confirmed the continuation of our food source. And light years above us, the stars winked with the infinite wisdom that we'd always be together.

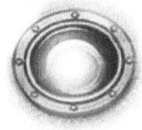

Electrons are Mocking You

By Jon Wesick

Veiled in quantum weirdness,
they thumb their noses
at your reality.

Standing in front of your face,
they'll kick you in the ass.
Pie fights, head bonks,
noses caught in pliers—
they could be up to anything down there.

Know this! Each pen, Brazil nut,
and speck of dust contains
 trillions
   of trillions
     of stooges
laughing behind your back.

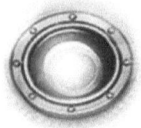

Quantum Entanglement

by Robin Pond

In the older suburban neighborhood, late at night, all the houses are in complete darkness except for one. As Hope paces, her shadow is visible on the curtains. She's wearing her nightgown, a look of grim determination on her face. She glances over at her reflection in the hall mirror. Recently she has noticed more lines. She looks paler, drawn, more tired than she used to. Despite Ernest's claim, time marches on. She doubts he, or any other mortal, can really bend it to his will.

The only sound is the ticking of the grandfather clock, a wedding gift from Ernest's Aunt Florence, who had chosen it especially because she knew Ernest did something or other with time, although she remained vague on the details.

Hope stares at the clock's ornate face, the sun and moon and stars all in gold, chasing each other over the dark cherrywood background. It's just past one. Too many dinners alone. Too much time squandered in this rambling house. Too much of her life measured out by that damned relentless rhythmic ticking, like drops of water cascading in a measured single-file down on to her consciousness.

The darkened hallway is illuminated by the lights of an approaching car. Hope darts over to the rolltop desk and yanks down the cover. She switches off the light, draws a deep breath, and then proceeds as planned, into the front hallway and up the stairs.

A door creaks open, and Ernest, a conservatively dressed man in early middle-age, slips inside. He's aging much more graciously than she is. Another source of resentment. He creeps to the foot of the stairs. As he places a foot on the bottom step, Hope switches on the hall light. She's standing above him on the landing, arms crossed, glaring down at him like a judge about to pass sentence.

"I thought I saw a light on. Sorry—"

"Do you know what time it is?" Hope has already heard far too many apologies.

He shrugs. "I guess I lost track."

Hope starts down the stairs. "Easy to do when you're spending all your time with the love of your life."

He studies her as she comes down the stairs, unsure whether she is serious or kidding.

"What are you talking about? You know I was in the lab."

"That's exactly what I'm talking about."

Ernest steps back, and when Hope arrives in the hall in front of him, he bends in to kiss her.

She draws back. "I've been doing a lot of thinking, Ernie, while sitting here all alone, as usual, and—"

"Why don't we go up to bed?"

"We need to talk."

Ernest sighs. He knows how difficult it is to wrap up one of their talks once they get started, and he has a full day planned for tomorrow. His shoulders slump. Even though he knows trying to avoid such a talk, or even trying to defer it, is a strategy doomed to failure, still he tries.

"Yeah, sure. I love talking to you. You know that. But it's so late. Maybe this isn't a good time."

"For a guy who spends his life studying time, why is it there never seems to be a good time with you? I'd give anything for a good time. I deserve a good time, too!"

"That's why I thought if we went right to bed, we could, you know, cuddle for a bit. And I need to get some sleep. I've got an early morning..."

With a scream, she grabs him and shakes him, protesting his lack of empathy. He's now in damage control, telling her how sorry he is, how important she is to him, how important she will always be, much more important than his work. His reassurance continues for some time.

Then a few seconds of stony silence, and finally she says, "And yet you're never here. It's your work that's all-consuming."

They slip into their well-worn argument, with Ernest responding defensively, the way he always does.

"You've always known how important my work is to me."

She seems to soften. "I know. I'm not blaming you. But I don't want to end up being just one more thing consumed by your work."

"I know. I completely understand. I promise I'll try—"

"We're way passed trying!" And then after another icy pause, "It's time we did something about it."

"Sure...why don't we plan a nice dinner, a date night, this coming Saturday?"

"No. Now. Not later. No time like the present."

"Actually, there may be multiple times, possibly infinite times, just like the present."

Hope merely groans with disgust and marches into the living room. He is forced to follow her in. She reaches up beside the grandfather clock and flicks the light back on before continuing into the middle of the room. She turns to face him and pauses. She is determined to calmly make her case, but over the next several minutes, their conversation falls into the same well-worn path.

Ernest resorts to his usual defense. "You've always loved how passionate I am about my work. Remember? That's why you were attracted to me in the first place."

"Yeah, live and learn. I was young, and I foolishly assumed the passion I saw in you would spill over to everything else, including me... especially me. But it doesn't work like that. It's exclusive, not inclusive. The more passion you expend at work, the less remains for me. And I'm tired of it. I'm lonely. I want to be someone's all-consuming passion."

And then he's back to telling her how sorry he is, but she tells him she isn't blaming him. She now realizes that's just who he is. Her resignation is a new feature in their argument. She has never been this accepting.

"But it's not like I'm cheating on you. I mean, not with another woman, or anything like that."

She laughs. "That might be easier to cope with. I could compete with that."

"You don't really mean that."

"No?"

He takes hold of her. "You've got to know, Hope, for me there'll never be anyone else. I really do love you."

"I believe you." She stares into his eyes, fighting the urge to abandon her plan. "Trouble is, you love time more."

"I'll make more of an effort. I promise. To be here for you. To spend time. Just the two of us. We'll plan a whole weekend...as soon as I can get away."

She pulls away from him. "Talk about a temporal loop."

"What?"

"How many times have we been right here, having this conversation?" She plants her feet and crosses her arms with the demeanor of a prosecutor tearing apart the defendant's testimony. "How many times have you promised it'd be different in future? And it always ends up the same."

"You're right. We're stuck in a groove. Next you're going to tell me about your parents, how they wasted their lives staying together after the love turned into resentment. But we're not them."

Hope remembers sitting on the couch, cringing. Her mother and father standing on either side of her, flinging insults and recriminations. Her mother pointing out what a useless loser her father is, how he always squanders all their money. Her father calling her mother a judgmental bitch, saying nothing he does is ever good enough.

Hope shoves aside the memories. "I'm still not prepared to waste my life. Just going 'round and 'round. We've got to break free, once and for all."

Ernest, frightened by her resolve, goes back to promising to focus less on work and more on her.

"That's not what I want," she says.

"It isn't?"

"No. Of course not." She takes his hands in hers, her eyes watery. "Look, Ernie, you're a remarkable man. Someday you'll probably achieve greatness, become famous, just because of how absorbed you get in all those temporal concepts. And I don't want to get in the way of that."

"So you don't want me to scale back my work?"

"Not at all."

"Then what do you want?"

"I don't want *you* to have a different life. I want *me* to have a different life."

He regards her, warily. "But you've got your own job, your own interests."

"But it's all so limited...so lonely. Our being together has closed off so many other possibilities. It's kept me from developing into who I really want to be."

Ernest reaches out to embrace her. "Nonsense. You're very much your own person, a person I love very much."

Hope pulls away again. "No. It's too late. And if you love me, you'll help me to escape."

"I'm not sure I see—"

"You've told me you believe you've got the ability to affect the past, right?"

"Yes. Retro-causality."

"So we can travel back in time and undo things, change events?"

"It's not really time travel." Ernest's manner becomes more professorial. "That's the mistake people make, thinking we can travel through time in a spatial sense. There are physical barriers to—"

"Yeah, yeah, I know. But it's possible to affect the past?"

"Yes. Like I've told you, the essential insight is in realizing that the additional dimensions predicted in string theory are temporal rather than spatial. Every moment of our lives presents a juncture to countless future possibilities, like a prism refracting light."

"But we can choose which path we take through that prism, right?"

He shrugs. "That's the exciting part. This may be a verifiable theory. While it's still highly experimental at this point, I believe it's possible to transmit thought, awareness, back through time. The past is memory, and with the right mixture of ions in the right medium, chemical enhancement for our neural receptors, we can affect past memories by opening up the channels which permit us to consciously implant new thoughts, and when this new awareness becomes integrated into our memories, it can affect our past actions, and that will change our personal histories."

"Right. Then make it happen."

"Make what happen?"

Hope moves closer to him. "Remember our first meeting, at the orientation party at the beginning of my first semester?"

"Of course I do." He smiles. "It was love at first sight."

"I want us not to go to that party. I want us never to have met there."

His eyes widen in horror. "Hope! No!"

"You promised. That very first night. You committed to giving me anything I wanted."

"But—"

"And this is what I want."

"Surely there's some other way. Some sort of compromise. I understand you're feeling a little down at this point, a little depressed, maybe a bit bored. I know. I get it. But maybe if you just get involved in some new project or hobby or—"

"No! You don't get it! You never do!"

"I'm trying, Hope. I really am."

She takes a deep breath, and then continues in a quieter tone. "I know you are. And I do love you for it. But this isn't a problem you can simply solve, Ernie. It's not just a phase I'm going through. And there's no magic equation that's going to make me feel more fulfilled. I've given this a lot of thought. This isn't what I want. I want another chance, a different life."

"It's not that simple."

But she has already walked over to the rolltop desk. She pulls the cover back. There are two glasses inside, each with a murky bluish liquid.

"Sure it is. I've already prepared the serum."

"But how—?"

She chuckles. "This is all you ever talk about. You didn't think I knew exactly how to prepare it?"

"But altering the past has serious consequences."

"Yes. I know. That's what I'm counting on." She picks up the two glasses from the desk and hands one to him. "Please. For me. It's what I really want. Drink a toast with me to a different yesterday, providing me with an altered tomorrow."

Ernest realizes he could never deny Hope anything, not even this. He looks at her, sadly.

"I guess this'll be goodbye, then."

She kisses him softly. "Goodbye, my love."

The grandfather clock gongs. It's1:30.

"If this is really what you want..."

"It is."

"You're sure?"

"Yes. Completely. We have to make it so we never meet at that orientation party."

They both drink the serum, then put down the glasses and join hands.

Hope says, "I won't go to the orientation party."

Ernest says, "I won't go to the orientation party."

And together they repeat, "I won't go to the orientation party...I won't go to the orientation party..."

Inside their heads, along neural pathways, there is an explosion of activity.

And then their reality dissolves.

ΩΩΩ

The room is crowded with young coeds, feverishly enjoying the party. Loud music, talking, laughing. A few on one side of the room are dancing. Over on the other side, closer to the entrance, Hope, a young woman in a bright blue dress, is seated on one of the chairs, surveying the proceedings. She looks around nervously, expectantly. Ernest, wearing a tweed jacket and khakis, strolls into the room. When he spots Hope, he stops and stares, his mouth ajar.

She catches his stare and returns it with an ironic smile. After a hesitation, he quickly joins her.

"Uh...hi there. I don't believe we've met. I'm Ernest."

She examines him. "Hope."

After an awkward handshake, he motions to the seat beside her. She shrugs, and he interprets this as a sufficient invitation. He sits beside her, and battling the loud music, asks her all about herself. She's a first-year undergraduate still searching for a major. He's a graduate student in physics. They both express surprise at having never seen the other before.

"I was planning on attending the orientation at the beginning of term," he said, "but something came up."

"Yeah, I didn't go to that one, either."

They run out of the usual introductory topics, and he leans close to her to be heard over the blaring music.

"This is going to sound lame, but..."

She looks at him curiously. "What?"

"When I saw you sitting here, just now, from across the room. It's like—I don't know—like I felt we were connected. Sort of like, well...there's this concept called quantum entanglement. Do you know what that is?"

"Is that when you get your quantums all messed up together?" Hope laughs, but only gets a blank stare from Ernest.

For some reason, he feels a desperate need to explain, as if his whole future depends on it.

"It's sort of like an invisible force connecting particles. When one spins a certain way, the other spins in sympathy. It doesn't matter whether they're together or far apart, there's this invisible bond. I think the two of us are like that."

"Both spinning?"

He continues in the same serious, pleading tone. "Both interconnected, attracted, in sync, moving in tandem, on some indiscernible level."

After a pause, she says, "You're right."

"You think so?"

"Yeah. It does sound lame." But he appears so deflated, she says, "Does this line often work for you?"

"No." He still looks dejected. "I mean, it's not a line. I honestly believe it."

She studies him. "You're really into all this quantum physics stuff?"

He brightens. "Absolutely. My thesis is going to be on *time*."

"That's better than handing it in late."

"No. The study of time. Interconnections between past, present, and future. I'm convinced it's possible to break free from the chains of time, from slavishly marching from yesterday to today to tomorrow in a totally restricted, linear, unidirectional manner."

"And how do you do that?"

His voice becomes conspiratorial. "The key is in the mind."

"You mean, time is just a mental construct?"

"Sort of." He leans oppressively close to her, gripping the back of her chair. "You see, our past and present and future are all encoded in our minds as memory and perception and premonition. It's dynamic, constantly changing with learning, establishment of new neural networks, and reinforcement of pathways, and with active forgetting and entropy. But the point is, it's all there, together, all at the same time. And so it should be possible to cross back and forth between the various states, between perception and memory, to free ourselves from the strict ordering of temporal events."

Hope leans back, trying to establish more personal space. "That sounds totally crazy."

Ernest slumps back into his own chair. "Yeah, I guess it does."

"But I love the way you talk about it."

"You do?"

"I do." She smiles at him. "Are you always so passionate when you talk about your work?"

"I guess so." He nods. "I'm always surprised others don't find these concepts as captivating as I do."

Hope's smile broadens. "You mean, women don't throw themselves at your feet when you tell them all about the space-time continuum?"

"Sadly, no." He returns her smile. "But they should. A man who can control space and time can give you anything you desire."

"And can you give me whatever I desire?"

"I honestly believe that's what I'm meant to do. And I'd love to spend a lifetime trying."

Hope tilts her head. "There'll probably come a time when I regret this, but...okay." She stands and takes him by the arm, drawing him up out of his seat. "C'mon. Let's go find a quiet spot so we can spend more time exploring our quantum entanglement."

ΩΩΩ

The grandfather clock in the living room gongs. It's 1:30. An older bedraggled Hope stands there, holding her glass of bluish liquid, determination oozing from her pores.

Ernest, also holding a glass, appears defeated. "If this is really what you want..."

"It is."

"You're sure?"

"Yes. Completely. We have to make it so we never meet at that end-of-term party."

They both solemnly drink. They put down the glasses and join hands.

Hope says, "I won't go to the end-of-term party."

Ernest says, "I won't go to the end-of-term party."

And together they repeat, "I won't go to the end-of-term party...I won't go to the end-of-term party..."

Inside their heads, along neural pathways, there is an explosion of activity.

And then their reality dissolves.

ΩΩΩ

A crowded coffee shop, late in the afternoon. There is a long line of people waiting at the counter. Every table is occupied, some by groups talking, and some by collections of individuals reading or checking their phones or working on laptops. Hope, a young coed dressed in jeans and a t-shirt, is seated at a small table, reading *Slaughterhouse Five*. The young woman sitting opposite her gets up and leaves, and Ernest, wearing his trademark tweed jacket and khakis, comes by carrying his coffee.

He motions to the empty chair. "Do you mind?"

"Suit yourself."

"It's always so crowded in here." Ernest sits. "I usually just grab my coffee and leave, but for some reason, today..."

Hope has already gone back to reading.

He stares at her, trying to think of something else to say.

Finally, he says, "Is that a good book?"

She looks up. "Yeah, I'm really enjoying it."

"Yeah, I can tell." Ernest takes a sip of his coffee. "I'm totally envious. I never seem to have time to read for pleasure."

Hope tilts her head, looking him over. "You should make the time."

Ernest leans towards her. "Funny you should say that...about making time...cause in a way, that's my work. That's what I'm trying to do."

Hope sits straighter, sensing a strange attraction.

ΩΩΩ

The grandfather clock in the living room gongs. It's 1:30. An older Hope stands there, holding her glass of bluish liquid, determination oozing from her pores.

Ernest, also holding a glass, appears defeated. "If this is really what you want..."

"It is."

"You're sure?"

"Yes. Completely. We have to make it so we never meet in that coffee shop."

They both solemnly drink. They put down the glasses and join hands.

Hope says, "I won't go to that coffee shop in third year."

Ernest says, "I won't go to that coffee shop."

And together they repeat, "I won't go to that coffee shop...I won't go to that coffee shop..."

Inside their heads, along neural pathways, there is an explosion of activity.

And then their reality dissolves.

ΩΩΩ

The university library, in the early afternoon. A younger Hope, dressed in jeans and a blue plaid shirt, is working on an essay. She is typing into her laptop. Various books and papers are strewn around the table in front of her. She glances up to see Ernest, who is wearing his khakis and an identical blue plaid shirt.

"You've got great taste in shirts," he says.

She smiles. "So do you."

He slides into the chair next to her. "When I saw you, just now, sitting here, I knew I had to come over and introduce myself. I'm Ernest."

ΩΩΩ

Standing together in the living room, hand in hand, an older Hope and Ernest repeat, "I won't go to that library...I won't go to that library..."

Inside their heads, along neural pathways, there is an explosion of activity.

And then their reality dissolves.

ΩΩΩ

Standing together in the living room, hand in hand, an older Hope and Ernest repeat, "I'll never go to Cheryl's birthday bash...I'll never go to Cheryl's birthday bash..."

Inside their heads, along neural pathways, there is an explosion of activity.

And then their reality dissolves.

ΩΩΩ

Standing together in the living room, hand in hand, an older Hope and Ernest repeat, "I'll never go to that alumni dinner...I'll never go to that alumni dinner..."

Inside their heads, along neural pathways, there is an explosion of activity.

And then their reality dissolves.

ΩΩΩ

The grandfather clock in the living room gongs. It's 1:30. Hope and Ernest stand facing each other, each holding a glass of bluish liquid. Hope shivers. She starts to speak, but then swoons. Ernest sets his glass down on the coffee table and catches her. While supporting her weight, he takes the glass out of her hand and sets it down next to his.

"What's wrong?"

She shakes her head weakly, unable to respond.

He continues to support her. "Maybe you're not getting enough sleep, or there's something not quite right with your diet. Maybe you need vitamins."

Slowly, she recovers. "I just got the most overwhelming sense of déjà vu."

He nods. "Yeah, I know. Me, too. I was afraid of that."

"Afraid of what?"

He whispers, "I've always suspected déjà vu might be a side effect of retro-causality."

Hope pulls free from Ernest and regards him suspiciously. "So what does that tell you?"

"I'm not positive, but it could be we've already tried to not meet before."

"So it's not working?"

"Probably not."

She throws up her hands in frustration. "But you said we could change our past. You were so damned sure. You promised."

"I'm still sure. This doesn't prove we've failed to alter the past. But it's possible that no matter how much we change the past, we end up here, today, in the same present."

"Why? What's screwing us up?"

"Quantum entanglement."

"Not that again."

"It's a powerful force."

Hope gives him a sour look. "I know you've always believed in that, Ernie. That we're connected, meant for each other, or whatever. And it's a cute theory, but—"

"It's not just a theory. It's a verifiable fact. The way we're feeling right now could be considered empirical evidence. It's—"

"It's nonsense! That's what it is. You don't spin in the same direction I spin in at all. We're totally incompatible."

"But that doesn't prove we're not connected. It merely shows we're negatively correlated. Kind of like your parents."

"I've told you a thousand times, I don't want to end up like my parents!"

"Perhaps that's a bad example."

Hope narrows her eyes as she grapples with this new information.

She stares at the glasses on the coffee table. "So how do we break this connection?"

"I don't think we can." He puts his arm around her. "If my theory's correct, we'll keep finding each other."

Hope looks at him pleadingly. "But I don't want us to. I don't know how to make this any clearer. This is not what I desire."

He shakes his head. "Desire's got nothing to do with it."

"That's half the problem."

"Look, maybe we shouldn't try. I mean, rather than trying to sever the connection, maybe we should focus on trying to improve it."

He tries to embrace her, but again she pulls away.

"But I want to be free."

"Freedom is often illusory." He can't help slipping into his professorial demeanor. "Free will might be nothing more than just being unaware of the preordained outcome. You can change your yesterday all you want, but your tomorrow might still be predetermined."

A realization begins to take hold in Hope's mind. She again regards her husband with suspicion.

"Isn't that convenient, the future being predetermined to be just the way you want it to be?"

"It's got nothing to do with me or what I want."

"Doesn't it?"

"No. I'm not God."

"But you like to play the part. I've been such an idiot, looking to you to fix the problem, when you're part of it. You don't really want it fixed, do you? You're really not trying to eradicate this relationship, are you? Of course we're always going to keep meeting—"

"That's not fair. I've done everything in my power—"

"When we're implanting our thoughts on our past lives, your thoughts still want us to be together, don't they?"

"No."

"Really?"

"Not consciously."

"Aha! I knew it." Hope steps up to the coffee table and grabs the glasses, one in each hand. "Ending a relationship is a solitary action. How can we take action as a couple, to cease being a couple?"

"Hope, don't do anything rash. Think about what you're doing." But he knows nothing he says will dissuade her.

"I'm going to see to it we never connect, never have that first conversation."

She gulps down the serum from one glass, and then the other. She stiffens, smiling at him triumphantly.

"Whenever I see you, I'm going to scream and run from the room...I'm going to scream and run from the room..."

Her eyes widen. She collapses.

Inside her head, along neural pathways, there is an explosion of activity.

And then her reality dissolves.

ΩΩΩ

Another late night in the lab. Ernest, older and more disheveled, and wearing a white lab coat, is watching a mouse run through a maze, and checking the results from the neural implants being recorded on his laptop. His hair is unkempt and he has a scruffy beard. He's so focused on his work that his graduate student has to say *excuse me* multiple times before he finally looks up. She explains that there is a woman here from the alumni board, but he tells her it's not a good time and to schedule a meeting for another day.

But before the graduate student can relay the message, a mature, stylishly dressed Hope appears beside her.

"Sorry for the interruption, Dr. Burston, but this should just take a moment. I'm Hope Givens, from the alumni society."

Ernest stares at Hope, his mouth ajar. "Sure. No problem." He nods and waves the graduate student away. "I'm sure I can spare a few moments...as long as you need."

"Thanks." Hope smiles. "The reason I'm here..." She makes a guttural moan and looks down, steadying herself on the lab table. "What a strange sensation...I...I..." She glances back up at Ernest, and then screams uncontrollably.

She is still emitting this ear-piercing sound of terror as she races from the lab.

Ernest watches her retreat. "What an outrageous reaction. Totally insane."

The graduate student apologizes and promises to keep the crazies out of the lab in the future, but he assures her it is not her fault.

He returns to his work, checking the results, but still distracted. *There's something about that lady, though. Sort of alluring, in a crazy never-know-what-you're-going-to-get kind of way.*

He examines his equipment. Checks one of the graphs, and notes an observation while still mulling over the strange behavior of that mysterious woman.

I should find out her name. Maybe we could get together sometime.

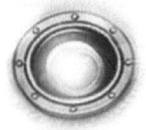

Expecting

by Teresa Trent

"And that is the final piece." Candace stepped back, her gaze drifting across the baby's room.

It looked like a picture out of *Modern Mother Magazine*. Blue and yellow accent colors were picked up in the bedding, curtains, rug, and an exquisite robin's egg blue rocker Candace found on sale. This had become her favorite room in the house. Sometimes she would slip in, sit in the rocker, and sing to the little one she was expecting.

Greg walked in with a large cardboard box. "Not quite. We got something from the fertility clinic."

Candace stared at the unopened carton. It was big enough to be a swing, or some other expensive necessity.

How sweet of them to send a baby gift. "Open it," she said.

Candace and Greg had wanted to have a baby for years, but were heartbroken when they found out they were unable to on their own. Adoption was always an option, but Candace wanted to give birth so bad she refused to think of it. She wanted to be pregnant, to have cravings, and to enjoy feeling that little person inside of her. Friends and family suggested invitro fertilization, but there was never enough money to afford fertility treatments.

One day, after trying yet another combination of vitamins and ovulation times, Candace had attempted to hide the tears after another month of failed conception. While losing that battle, she was fumbling for her keys when she dropped them in the parking lot of her obstetrician's office.

"Here, let me help." A young woman in a crisp light blue suit bent over to pick up the keys.

"Thank you."

"I couldn't help noticing you're upset. Is there anything I can do?"

Candace gave a weak smile, embarrassed, and wanting to run away and mourn her loss alone.

"No. Not unless you can make a barren woman conceive a child."

It was an inappropriate conversation to have with a stranger, but her emotions had gotten the better of her. The woman blinked and her eyes widened. Light green. Not hazel, but a true green, like spring grass. Candace felt it wouldn't be so bad if she sank into quicksand.

Finally, the woman said, "You're going to think this is strange, but I think we were meant to run into one another today."

Candace tightened the grip on her keys and took a step back.

"Hear me out. I was just in the doctor's office myself, and…"

Is she another patient? Will she ask me for money next?

"I probably shouldn't be talking to you like this, but…hi. My name is Kyra." She extended a hand, and Candace shook it. "I represent a fertility clinic." She pulled a black business card out of her pocket.

An embossed silver starburst was on it, with the name *Cassiopeia Consultants* underneath.

"Thanks, but no. I'm a preschool teacher, and my husband is a salesman. We could never afford your services." Candace started to walk away.

"Even if we offered them on a sliding scale?" There was a twinkle in her eyes. Those green eyes. "Our firm is about people. Not profit. We feel we were put on this earth to make a difference. We want to change people's lives. Make the world a better place."

It all seemed too good to be true. A sliding scale? A company who saw them as people, not cash grabs that bankrupt loving couples?

That was how it all began. And as Candace now ran her hand over her pregnant belly, she was thankful for her chance-meeting with Kyra in the parking lot. The staff at *Cassiopeia* offered a caring experience in their state-of-the-art clinic, and the sliding scale was more than reasonable. It *was* as if they were meant to meet that day.

She focused on the unopened box. "Let's see what's inside."

"Can't," Greg said. "It says right here, we are not to open it until after the baby is born. They're pretty adamant about it, too. Big red letters on every side of the box."

"Really?" Candace took the box and shook it.

Whatever it was, there were a lot of little pieces.

"Fine. Just put it over there, and we'll open it when we bring the baby home."

And that was where it stayed for two more weeks. The baby, who Greg and Candace named Georgie, was born without a hitch. Natural delivery, baby blue eyes, excellent APGAR scores, and although he didn't take to mother's milk, he was able to digest formula. A lot of formula. Georgie was hungry all the time. He cried more than most babies.

A day after they arrived home from the hospital, Kyra called.

"I hear congratulations are in order."

Georgie was crying in the background, and Candace strained to hear. She was exhausted.

"Thank you."

"Did you get the gift we sent?"

The forgotten box still rested in the corner.

"Yes."

"I hope you haven't opened it?"

"No, no. We followed your instructions."

"Great. You may open it now, and be sure to read the card. Call me after, okay?"

"Sure."

After Candace hung up, she decided to ignore Georgie for just one more minute and tore open the box. What could they have sent with so many tiny pieces? Maybe it was some sort of building block toy to stimulate his intellect? Some type of brain enrichment?

As Candace lifted the flaps, she noticed a metallic bag taped at the top that crunched in her hand when she attempted to open it. She reached into the bag and pulled out tiny metal filings. A cockroach wing rested in the middle of silver and copper shavings. She threw it back in the box. What was this? Some kind of joke?

A black envelope with the now-familiar starburst lay on top. She tore it open and read.

Dear Candace and Greg,

Congratulations on your new baby. While helping you create your life-changing event, we added a few genetically superior extras. We think our brand of infant formula will help your little one grow strong and intelligent. Simply add a teaspoon to each bottle of formula.

Cassiopeia Consulting

Changing Earth One Person at a Time

Candace looked over at Georgie, who had become quiet. Then he gave her a toothless grin, and she realized his baby blue eyes had turned light green.

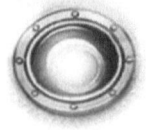

Coding

by Terry Sanville

1.

Sasha adjusted her helmet, then reached for the water bottle. She'd been peddling hard for forty minutes, gaze focused on the county road that wound among the sunbaked vineyards. A third of the way through her ride, she pulled up at the top of a long hill and leaned her bicycle against an oak. The summer wind off the Pacific smacked her in the face.

While sitting on the ground, with her knees drawn up, she retrieved her smartphone and selected an app that connected with her Continuous Glucose Monitoring (CGM) device. She'd been an insulin-dependent diabetic for all of her forty-two years. The device, a small box worn at her waist and connected to a tiny needle inserted in her belly, made it easy for her to track her blood sugar levels and stay out of trouble.

The back of her neck felt numb, and dark spots appeared before her eyes. *Damn, I always run out of steam right about here.* She keyed the phone application, but the number that appeared—132—didn't make any sense. She expected a low blood sugar reading, something less than fifty, since she'd exercised vigorously and had eaten a light lunch. But the CGM showed a slightly above normal number. She should feel fine. But she didn't.

Maybe I'm just buzzed from climbing those hills. I did push myself. Kevin's been kidding me about my hips...like he should talk. Sasha sucked in deep breaths, slow and steady, forcing her muscles to relax and her heartbeat to return to its at-rest pace. But her vision continued to dim, and the numbness in her neck crept down her spine and across her shoulders. *Fuck it, I gotta treat it as a low...even though the CGM shows it's close to normal.*

Sasha fumbled with the sealed packet of glucose gel, ripped it open with her teeth, and sucked down the super-sweet jelly. The grape flavoring made her gag. The light continued to fade and all feeling went out of her legs. She felt exhausted and leaned back against the oak's rough bark. Her mind danced like a lightning bug, blinking on and off as it skittered through the New England skies of her childhood.

She reached inside her jersey and pulled out a can of pineapple juice. After popping the pull-tab, she chugged it and finished just before darkness closed in and purple-tinged dreams took her away.

A passing motorist tooting his car horn brought her back. Her head felt fuzzy, and she struggled to stand and shake the circulation back into her limbs. She checked her watch. About twenty-five minutes had passed since she'd stopped. Her blood sugar level now read above normal—212. *What the hell's going on? Can't depend on these damn machines.*

Kevin had made her get the CGM as a safety feature for bicycling alone. She remembered when they first married and rode through the Central Coast backcountry. They'd find a secluded field or quiet spot under the sycamores and make love with the red-tailed hawks screeching their approval. But Kevin had developed a heart rhythm problem that required a pacemaker to keep it beating. He got scared and stopped riding. Now both of them depended on machines.

Feeling drained of strength, Sasha mounted her bike and rode home slowly. After entering their hillside house, she dug her old testing kit out of a junk drawer and pricked her finger with a lancet for a blood sample. The handheld meter showed a reading of 110, while the CGM showed 108—both in the normal range. *Something's screwy with my machine.*

She heard the front door rattle. Kevin pushed inside, lugging his golf bag and muttering to himself. The color drained from his face when he saw her.

"Jesus, Kevin, I don't look that bad, do I?"

"No, no of course not. I'm...I'm just surprised to see you home so early. Your Saturday rides usually take all afternoon."

"Yeah, well I had problems in the valley. Had a low blood sugar episode. A bad one."

"Isn't your CGM supposed to trigger an alarm when it drops too low?"

"Yes, that's what puzzles me. It looks like it's out of whack."

"Better let me check it out." He extended a hand toward her. "I can hack into the phone app and see what's—"

"Hey, I'm as good a hacker as you. A bit rusty, but I can handle it."

"You're kidding me, right? You haven't written code in years. Here, give me the damn meter and I'll have it fixed this afternoon."

"Screw you, buddy."

"Okay, okay, you don't need to get pissed. But if ya need help, let me know."

Kevin worked for a struggling software and application design firm in San Francisco, but did all his work from their Paso Robles home, at night after Sasha had gone to bed. She knew he could fix any glitches in her CGM system, but she wanted to try herself, to regain some of the self-confidence she'd lost over the years while living with Kevin.

"I'm going out again," he called, from his office. "Gonna have a drink downtown with a potential client."

"Okay. Will you be home for dinner?"

"I don't think so. Better order out. You know how old businessmen need convincing. They barely know what the *cloud* is."

"Text me if you're going to be late."

"Will do."

The front door slammed, and the sound of his Honda faded into the distance.

Same old bullshit story. How long does he think I'll believe him?

Sasha moved to the sofa and watched a crummy movie on the classic TV channel. After downing a couple Pop-Tarts, a glass of Cabernet, and injecting herself with some fast-acting insulin to handle the sugar load, she retired to her computer and her smartphone. In less than an hour, she had retrieved the code for the interface between her cell and the CGM. She studied each line, working into the night.

Kevin returned and mumbled something she didn't catch. She smelled the scent of the other woman mingling with his sweat and dried semen. She said nothing. She had known about the affair for months. Her friends in the Book Club told her they'd seen him at restaurants with a female companion. *All such a damn cliché.*

Sasha hacked into her husband's email account. Kevin didn't know she could read his encrypted messages and their attachments. He hadn't even bothered to hide the emails to his mistress—kept them in a folder labeled *escape route*. She could guess where that name might've come from. Their prenup stipulated that if he got caught committing adultery, he would give up all claims to the estate, the majority of which had been Sasha's family money.

She read through the email folder, the steamy notes about where they wanted to rendezvous and what he wanted to do with her. Sasha poured herself another glass of wine and sat reading the latest words between the secret lovers, how they planned to meet at a remote trailhead the next Saturday, hike into the mountains to lie in the grass and fuck. She wept, her body shaking. But her tears turned to white flashes of anger that grew into rage. Even with all her efforts to keep herself fit and attractive, to pay attention to him, to support his ideas, he had drifted away.

She gulped some wine and returned to her analysis of the code for her CGM. Several lines looked funny. She had a gut feeling they didn't belong.

Over the next week, she experimented with using the device with the strange coding eliminated and with it re-installed, under various blood sugar conditions. By Thursday, she couldn't ignore the results of her analysis. When her blood sugar dropped below 50, an alarm should sound. It didn't. But more frightening, when the levels dropped below 50, the CGM added 100 points to the reading, making it look like her blood sugar levels were fine or slightly elevated. Some skilled coder had messed with her cell phone app, and that someone was Kevin.

She thought about confronting him, maybe even going to the police. *But the creep will just deny it, even though his motive for offing me is obvious.*

2.

Lauren waited at the airport bar. In the mirror she watched Kevin enter the room, smile, and move next to her. She wore her hair down, the blond mane spreading across her back like a carpet. Kevin liked carpets. He slid onto the stool and glanced sideways. She turned and planted a wet kiss on his lips. *That should get his motor running.*

"I'm glad you came," she said. "I was worried after...after our plan failed. You think your wife suspects?"

"I can't tell. We haven't been talking much."

"Yeah, I get that."

"Have you had lunch?" He slid an arm around the waistband of her stylish jeans.

"Yes. Let's get the hell out of here. Airports always make me worry."

"Why?"

"I don't know. Maybe because my dad left at an airport and never came back. You're not gonna leave me, are you, Kevin?"

He flashed her his little boy grin. "Hell no."

She gulped the remainder of her beer. Kevin dropped some bills on the counter. They took her Jeep and drove west across the freeway and into the mountains. After turning off onto a rutted dirt track, they wound uphill for miles until reaching the trailhead's empty parking area. Some idiots had blasted the National Forest Service signs with buckshot.

After getting out, she pulled her backpack from the car and they headed north along the ridge trail. She kept the pace slow. Her mind drifted to his body and what they planned on doing in the shade of the ancient moss-covered oak, the one with their initials carved into its trunk. The wine bottles clinked in her backpack. She hoped the cheese wouldn't spoil in the heat before they got there.

They walked for an hour with the trail to themselves. *Couldn't be more perfect. I'm so turned on I could jump him right here and now.*

Near the bottom of a deep notch in the ridgeline, they turned off and followed a deer trail downslope to a tiny bench on the side of the ravine. A massive oak stood guard over the narrow valley. She moved into the shade and removed her pack, spread a blanket across the thick bed of leaves and unpacked the wine. She poured Kevin an inch-worth into his plastic cup, wanting to slow him down, but not too much.

"How did you find this place?" he said.

"I had a boyfriend in high school who—"

"You don't need to tell me more. I get it."

"Relax. I'm not a competition, ya know."

"I know that." He grinned. "But you're young and hot. I get nervous."

They sipped the wine and stared into the valley, at the oak-covered slopes. Buzzards circled the golden fields far below. On the hillsides, the cones of the gray pines crackled, dropping their seeds into the arid landscape. Kevin lay back with his head in her lap, and she stroked his hair, thick for a fortyish guy. His breathing slowed and deepened.

Jesus, he could fade on me. She removed her top, yanked off her boots, and struggled out of her tight jeans and panties. A hot breeze caressed her nakedness. She felt like a little girl again, streaking past sand dunes in Mexico, with the Pacific's waves running up the beach to catch her.

Kevin stripped off his clothes and lay before her. After oral introductions, she mounted her stallion and took off at a slow trot that turned into a canter, then a full gallop. Their cries drowned out the racket made by the hawks and chasing crows. Afterward, they lay side-by-side, silent and covered in sweat. She listened to his breathing. It had a strange rattle to it and grew faster as she listened, as if he were still in the throes of lovemaking. Then it stopped.

Lauren waited a few seconds then bolted upright. Kevin's eyes fixed on the sky, unblinking, his face pale.

She gave him a shake. "Kevin, stop fooling around."

The crows continued to caw. She checked for a pulse in his neck and wrist, but couldn't find one. Straddling his body, she began CPR, trying to remember where to place her hands, how hard to push, and how fast. She kept at it until the pain in her arms and back forced her to stop. She checked his neck artery but still found no pulse. She reached over and snatched her cell phone from her jeans. But there was no reception in the narrow valley. She'd have to climb back up to the ridge trail...and leave Kevin.

The naked man lying beneath her had turned a light blue. She continued CPR until, exhausted, she fell across him. He felt cold. Sobs shook her body. Trembling, she rose to her feet.

"Help! We need help!"

After struggling into her clothes, she took off up the deer trail. She reached the ridgeline in half an hour and breathlessly called 911.

"What is your emergency?"

"My friend has died."

"Where are you and what happened?"

She explained everything to the dispatcher. The woman promised to send a rescue team to her location.

"I'm...I'm afraid it's too late." She sobbed.

"Just stay calm and stay put. A sheriff's unit will meet you on the ridge trail in a short while."

Lauren shuddered, dropped to the ground, and crouched in the shade of a Manzanita bush. She felt parched and cursed herself for leaving all the supplies back at the...the site. She gazed westward to the blue horizon and the ocean.

What the hell do I do now? They'll find him lying there naked, the cops will tell his wife, my name will be dragged through the mud. If his heart gave out, they might even charge me with something. Why do I always fall for the married ones. I'm such a cliché.

3.

A week after Kevin's cremation and internment, somebody banged on Sasha's front door. She set her wine glass down, turned off the TV, and answered it. A youngish man in a Brooks Brothers suit introduced himself.

"Sorry to bother you, ma'am. I'm Assistant Coroner Steve Jenkins, from the County Sheriff's Department. I have your husband's autopsy results, and I'd like to talk to you about them."

"Please, come in. Would you care for some wine?"

Sasha hated being called *ma'am*, but appreciated the young man's good looks.

"No, sorry, I'm on duty." His face reddened.

She ushered him into the living room. "Do you always hand-deliver autopsy results to the grieving widow? You could have mailed them to me and my insurance carrier."

"Yes, that would be the normal procedure. But I wanted to talk with you in person. There are some...some anomalies."

Sasha felt the back of her neck tingle. She slumped onto the sofa and stared into the coroner's eyes.

"What do you mean, anomalies?"

"Well, the deceased—I mean, your husband—died of cardiac arrest. In layman's terms, his heart stopped beating."

"Why would it do that?"

"We're not sure, and that's what puzzles us. The muscle itself looked to be in good condition. The arteries unobstructed, and the valves showed no deterioration. We thought at first that maybe his pacemaker had malfunctioned."

He stared into her eyes and seemed to be waiting for some reaction. Sasha fought to keep her breathing slow and steady. She sipped her wine.

"Did the damn thing fail, or what? If it did, I'll sue the manufacture if it's the last thing I—"

"Well, that's just it. We tested the pacemaker and it worked perfectly."

"Are there other cases where a pacemaker has failed?"

"Yes, but their circumstances don't seem to fit this situation."

"So now what?"

He cleared his throat. "We've listed COD—ah, cause of death—as cardiac arrest. I would have liked to study the remains some more, but of course that's impossible."

"Yes."

"We tested to see whether it might have been some allergic reaction to the medications he was taking, but found nothing conclusive."

"Anything else?"

"Well, no. I was hoping maybe you had some ideas. Maybe something in his medical history?"

Sasha shook her head, not trusting her voice. The silence built between them.

Finally, he stood. "I'm sorry to have taken up your time. If you have any questions, feel free to contact me." He extended a hand holding his business card, and hurried from her home.

Sasha moved to her computer and rechecked her folders, making sure all the research she'd done had been expunged. It had been easy hacking the Wi-Fi connection to Kevin's pacemaker, and writing code to get it to turn off for thirty minutes after a sustained increase in his heart rate—like when making love.

Pure genius, I tell ya. She grinned. *Who's the better coder now?*

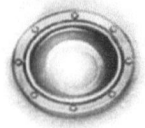

DETERMINED

BY TOM JOLLY

Benny Henderson looked down at the body. He'd stripped the space suit off the corpse, but it was burned beyond recognition. Sampling the DNA and comparing it with the ship's database had been his only recourse for identification.

"It's me. Well, damn." He looked up from the corpse on the table.

The other Bennies, over one hundred of them from earlier time loops, were long gone, already disappeared into the past, stepping one after another into the temporal displacement booth. They'd never even known about this body. He smiled, despite the evidence that he was going to die someday.

"This is why Hartwig thinks I died on this mission. This is why they didn't send anyone else."

And this was how he was going to stick it to them.

ΩΩΩ

"We want to send you back nine years," Jonathan Hartwig, the owner of Flying Gold, had told him.

The start-up asteroid mining company strove to stay afloat in a crowded pool of mining companies.

"It's part of our cost-saving effort to redistribute our assets to cover high-use periods, by time travelling from low-use periods. You cover two shifts, but each version of you is only working one shift, really."

An asset. Benny hated being referred to as an *asset*. Just a step up from *property*.

"So basically I'll be living through the same decade twice," he said.

Same crappy 2050s music, same news, same everything. He'd just be older and more tired.

"I knew this was coming. I met my future self a few years back."

"It will save us quite a lot on training costs. You know how much tech changes in a decade. At your age, your education is way behind the curve. You'd be much more comfortable with the tools and knowledge from the 50s. And we wouldn't have to let you go. It's fortunate that cycling one trained employee to cover multiple shifts and varying workloads within a single decade is so cost-effective."

There was the threat. Inevitable, Benny knew. It was the lever that assured the time loop was initiated.

"So I've been reading. How come there isn't some conflict with...uh..."

"Paradox? The idea that you can kill a young version of yourself, or give him information he wouldn't have unless he told it to himself?"

"Yeah. That."

Hartwig smiled. "Mr. Henderson, we live in a four-dimensional universe. What this means is that everything that happens to us already exists. We exist everywhere along our worldlines. That is, everywhere in time. The versions of you from a minute ago and a minute in the future exist and think, just as surely as we do now. It's totally deterministic. Paradox is impossible because everything that happens, every chance encounter with one's time travelling self, has already happened. The closed loop of interaction exists as a fixed loop in time, like a loop in a string. And just as certain chemical or subatomic reactions are impossible, certain structures in looped time also cannot exist."

Henderson frowned even deeper. "That's depressing as hell. You mean I don't have any choice in my future?"

"Certainly you do. But you always make the same choice at a given point in time, since the events leading to that decision never change."

"Uh-huh." He looked up at Hartwig. "And this is why gambling was outlawed when time-travel came about?"

"Of course. And why the creation of new information in a closed loop always results in the loss of the information before it can become an open loop—like an inventor failing to tell himself how to invent something. It's very...neat. Closed loops can't really affect externalities, so you can't kill yourself. Open loops, where all the information appears before the time loop starts, seem to function just fine."

"Cosmic censorship."

Hartwig shrugged. "That's the public catchphrase. But it's just physics."

ΩΩΩ

Benny Henderson met himself in a break room at the Ceres cargo dock. It had been during shift change. The other guy was twenty years older, sporting a gray goatee and a limp. Mostly bald, but there was no mistaking the similarity. Young Benny nodded to old Benny.

"So. I'm a time travelling cargo loader. For the next twenty years, looks like."

Old Benny gave a curt nod to young Benny. He saw the look in his eyes, the depression and resigned gloom of a predetermined future laid out before him, mapped in the man standing before him. He even remembered what he was about to tell himself.

"Yeah," old Benny said. "Twenty years. This is my second loop back. But you aren't going to believe what it's like." He forced himself to grin.

During the first loop back, he'd gone to great pains to avoid his younger self, just to avoid a meeting like this.

Young Benny grinned back. "So it's good? Give me a hint."

"It's good. Leave it at that. Why ruin the plot?"

"So if it's predetermined, I can do anything I want, right? Still got my job, still alive in twenty years. I could pull off my helmet in a vacuum and live through it, right?"

Old Benny thought about that time, floating in the vacuum, two kilometers from anything, when he thought about doing just that, just to see if he could do it, and chickened out. Just because he could do it didn't mean he wouldn't incur some brain damage and a world of pain recovering from it.

And what was it the old guy had said to him twenty years ago? Oh, yeah. "I wouldn't try that if I was you." He smirked.

If I was you—ha. He glanced down at his bad knee. Still the young version of himself was going to do some stupid things, knowing he was going to be alive in twenty years no matter what, like jumping off that cliff on Vesta. Dumbass. Well, he did rescue Angie that time, so hell. And that relationship had its ups and downs when she got a load of how reckless he was and the chances he kept taking all the time. Amazing she'd stuck with him all these years. Time traveler's wake, some called it. The ripples of chaos that a *determined* traveler causes to those around him.

"You'll have plenty of other excitement," he said.

Excitement didn't equal fun, of course, but no use telling him that. It was the flip side of being invulnerable. Your boss always used you as the canary in the mine, the first man in for truly dangerous situations. For the same reason that gambling ceased to exist, most potentially dangerous operations became tame. Yay, time travel.

He looked at young Benny staring at him, his wrinkles, the gimpy leg, the worn out cargo loader spelling out twenty years of his future boring life. And still a cargo loader, working the same job. He remembered the depression that overwhelmed the expectation of invulnerability. The stark desolation of a predetermined life. It weighed on some time travelers like a yoke of obligation.

"I don't know if I can do this," young Benny said.

Old Benny sighed. *Not like you have a choice, is it?* He sat, massaging his knee.

The low gravity helped a lot, but the joint still stiffened up in cold air.

"Benny, determination doesn't take away pleasure. You can still sit in the viewing room and enjoy a fine Martian Scotch after work. You can still read a good book, and you can still cuddle up with your woman when your shift is over. Just because your life is predetermined doesn't mean those pleasures you're going to have are any less pleasurable."

At the mention of *cuddling up with your woman*, young Benny's eyes brightened, as old Benny knew they would.

Old Benny stood. "Look, I got to start my shift, so maybe I'll run into you later. You're shipping out to Vesta tomorrow, aren't you?"

Young Benny nodded.

"Okay, I'll probably see you off." *For another pep talk so you won't feel so damn suicidal.*

It occurred to him that when he was young Benny, he lost track of his older self after about a year, assuming that he had been reassigned to Earth. Funny he never thought about that. Guess he'd find out soon enough where he took off to.

He left the room, thinking about the last twenty years. Gone so fast. He paused in the corridor and closed his eyes for a moment to clear the moisture from them. He didn't know what would happen if he met another version of himself, ten or twenty years older, doing the same damn job. Probably beat him to death. But then he'd remember that and avoid it, right?

ΩΩΩ

Benny stared at the float globes illuminating the office of the president of Flying Gold, Incorporated. The owner, Jonathan Hartwig, sat on the edge of his desk, looking down his nose at Benny.

"You've already looped once, haven't you?"

Benny grimaced and nodded, wincing at the monotony of the last few years.

"Four times. The last time was to double up for just a year."

"Even better. I'll cut to the chase here. We know there's a ship catastrophe that's going to happen next Tuesday, by Earth time, on a ship that's hauling out a billion tons of high-grade steel plates. A collision with a wayward asteroid."

Benny looked curiously at Hartwig. "That couldn't be avoided?"

Hartwig waggled his hands and rocked his head back and forth. "Not so simple. We have competitors with time travelers, too, you know. We think this asteroid has, or had, a fusion reactor rocket strapped to its hindquarters."

"Ah. And what am I supposed to do on this job?"

"Technically you're the most qualified loader for this ship type, and our other loaders are all on other jobs. We think we can get our ship unloaded before impact by moving the steel plates to drift in local space and retrieving them later, using only two hundred of you."

"You think...wait, what?"

"We need to loop you two hundred times. Make two hundred copies of you to unload the ship before impact. We'll have less than an hour to unload it by the time your ship gets there. Each looped copy of you will unload the ship, then return to the time machine to loop back to the start of the unload, and so on. We think this will take as many as a couple hundred of you, so maybe two hundred hours of your time. A few copies will have to be sleepers, but we've got that covered. We'll even pay for your sleep periods."

"And no one else is helping on this?"

Hartwig shrugged. "Like I said, they're on other assignments. Sending you by yourself is cost-effective." He fidgeted with the hem of his suit jacket.

Something was fishy. Why not send more help? Was the mission doomed somehow?

"You don't sound very sure about this. It's already happened, hasn't it? Determined already?"

Hartwig spread his hands. "We think we're running up against some of the information transfer blockages in time travel. We're not sure why. Maybe some virtual closed information loops."

"Hell."

ΩΩΩ

Benny's ship, the Ouroboros, arrived only four hours before the catastrophe was to occur. He wasted no time powering up the temporal displacement booth, and watched in awe as 136 copies of himself stepped out of the machine, one after the other. The later copies looked knowingly at the early versions, understanding what part of the job they'd already done.

The only version that hadn't already worked some part of the job was the one that had flown here in the ship—First Benny.

Copy number 136 popped out. "This is enough. Let's get it done." He put a red patch on his own sleeve to indicate that he was the eldest copy.

He'd already seen the work the other 135 had performed, so he knew 137 wasn't needed.

The others referred to 136 as *old man*. But he wasn't there to supervise, or even work. They secured him on the ship. He was the only copy that had no immunity to death. The only version that wouldn't step back into the time machine after an hour of work. Only the earliest version,

Copy 1, the one with no foreknowledge at all, was allowed to supervise. It was the only way they could avoid paradox—directing someone not to do something because you already knew he was going to do it.

The cargo ship Ampersand was drifting, its main engine destroyed three hours before by a small, high-velocity asteroid. There wasn't any doubt among the 136 copies of Benny that the engines had been targeted, and the small asteroid aimed. They could see a much larger asteroid, haloed by a fusion reactor exhaust plume behind it, headed toward the Ampersand's main body. It wasn't enough to just disable the ship. The person responsible for this attack wanted to spread its cargo across the solar winds.

The team worked quickly to offload the metals. They wore identical suits, so none of them knew who had foreknowledge. As they neared the end of the offload, the encroaching asteroid loomed as an ominous shadow against the stars. They packed up the cargo on the Ouroboros, then formed a queue to loop back in time. The younger versions of himself disappeared as though being eaten by the TDB. The youngest Benny nodded to Old Man Benny before he looped back. Then Old Man Benny peeled off his red armband and sighed. He moved the Ouroboros out of the potential debris field of the impending collision, poured himself a small dram of Scotch, and sat back to watch the show.

It gave him time to think. Why had his boss seemed so nervous? Did his boss think he was going to die on this job? Was that why he was the only guy sent out here. One old, worn-out spacer was expendable, but two was just too expensive? What was it that had already happened that scared Hartwig? Did everybody on his ship die? Is that why he only wanted to send one guy?

He swirled his whisky in his glass and pondered the problem. An idea formed in his head. And when the idea formed, a new loop closed.

Determination committed itself. Details filled out the idea. For it to work, he'd have to act as First Benny. He'd have to make all the first choices, and direct the future play.

There would have to be a dead Benny he could send back, one for Hartwig and the goons at Flying Gold to find. A body that could pass any identity test. A real Benny, from his own future, from the end of his future where he died. What he was planning now might take forty years to implement, maybe longer if he had a long life, and someone would have to send his corpse back to this moment and deliver it to him.

The ship's computer said, "Technician Henderson, there is an object headed at slow speed toward this ship. It appears to be a space suit. There is a heat signature of one-hundred-twenty-point-five degrees Celsius. It is currently ten-point-seven klicks away, and will pass within twenty meters of the ship in two minutes, twenty-three seconds."

Benny smiled and nodded. "Prepare the shuttle, and I'll bring it in."

When he pulled in the body, it was obvious no life was there. The suit was heat-blasted, still warm, and the face inside the suit was barely recognizable. Cooked meat.

"It's me. Well, damn."

But he would live through this, maybe for decades if he planned it right.

After peeling the suit from the corpse, he found the data chip he was looking for. It would have coordinates on it.

He knew he'd have to create a believable scenario where he died from some event that had cooked him. Cooked him well enough that they couldn't tell how old the body was, with its extra gray hair or balding pate, its manifold wrinkles, and the deep laugh lines around his eyes.

The Ouroboros wasn't a huge ship, and reactor core malfunctions weren't unheard of. He'd just have to leave the body behind, set the reactor to blow, and set the autopilot to return home. They wouldn't find much left of the ship's shuttle except for a few seats and internal panels, those that he could do without when he took off.

And that explained why Hartwig didn't want to send anyone else on this mission. He thought everyone on the ship was going to die. What a bastard.

There wouldn't be a lot of his corpse to find, either, but they'd find it. They'd analyze the DNA, and they'd pay off his widow. His wife would grieve, which was unfortunate, but he would contact her soon. The death benefits would have to support both of them, after all.

He wondered how long this *retirement* would last. But a lot of the details, how things were going to play out, would depend on the altruism of his new employers, the folks who'd attacked the Ampersand, the people who had assured that his death, when it finally came, would buy him some truly enjoyable years of life. But in exchange for what? He knew a hell of a lot about Flying Gold's operations. Would that be enough to make it worth their while?

After getting in the shuttle, he headed toward the coordinates taken from the chip on his corpse, and set the Ouroboros on its way with his body.

ΩΩΩ

When his shuttle arrived at the coordinates two days later, drifting dark with its engines powered down to stay hidden, a small transport ship appeared and took his shuttle on board.

There was only a single pilot as crew for the ship, and he introduced himself and gravely shook Benny's hand.

"When do I meet your boss?" Benny said.

The stranger stared at him for a moment, and then laughed. He stepped over to a steel cabinet, opened it and pulled out a bottle of golden liquid, then pulled out two glass cups and poured a bit into each cup. He handed one to Benny, taking the other for himself.

"My boss told me you might need this to clear the cobwebs."

Benny sniffed at the glass, then inhaled deeply. "Glen Marineris," he breathed.

The pilot winked at him and nodded. "First guess, boss."

Benny frowned as his brain finally started working. "I've got to let Angie know. She's going to think I'm dead."

"She already knows. We sent someone back to notify her after you left to offload the steel. Boss, it's been a pleasure...going to be a pleasure, working with you."

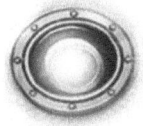

Are We Alone?

by Arthur M. Doweyko, PhD

"Two possibilities exist: Either we are alone in the Universe or we are not. Both are equally terrifying."
−*Arthur C. Clarke*

Okay, so I know all about the Drake equation and how probable it is that life exists in the rest of our galaxy as well as the universe. But you do realize that this is an exercise in probability based on a bunch of one in a thousand assumptions made up out of thin air—covering planet existence, location, makeup, the origin of life, length of viable civilization, and so on. In the end, it's just a probability—one which points to a universe teeming with life.

The problem is that the evidence that has indeed piled up is embarrassing. Maybe you've heard of the Great Silence.

Back in the 50s, physicist Enrico Fermi noted that there was a contradiction between the lack of evidence and such high-probability estimates for the existence of extraterrestrial civilizations. Main points: There are billions of stars in our galaxy that are similar to the sun, and many of these stars are billions of years older than our solar system. There is a high probability—Drake—that some of these stars have

Earth-like planets, and if the Earth is typical, some may have developed intelligent life. Furthermore, some may have developed interstellar travel. Even at sub-light speeds, the other life forms in our galaxy could have traversed its hundred-thousand-light-year diameter in a few million years.

The Earth should have been visited by extraterrestrial aliens by now. At the very least, we should have picked up radio transmissions. This Great Silence, also known as the Fermi Paradox, led Fermi to ask, "Where is everybody?"

There are a whole slew of arguments made to explain the paradox—we aren't listening properly, everyone is listening and no one is transmitting, Earth is deliberately ignored, it's too dangerous to communicate, and so forth.

So the question *Are We Alone?* has some merit, in that the possibility that we are alone is likely. And if so, some amazing questions come to mind.

Why such a big place—universe—for just our little planet?

What's the meaning of it all?

What's our purpose in being here?

Are we the start of life in the universe?

BIOGRAPHIES

Charles Joseph Albert works as a metallurgist in San Jose, and writes poetry and fiction on the trolley to and fro. His work has appeared recently in *Vallum, Write City, Amsterdam Quarterly, the Apeiron Review, The MOON*, and the *Lowestoft Chronicle*. His first novel, *The Unsettler*, is currently being released by *SERIAL Magazine*, and his third volume of poetry, *Confession to the Cockroaches and Other Poems*, has just been released by Dangeray Press.

Arthur M. Doweyko, PhD, writes science fiction and fantasy. As an internationally recognized scientist, he invented novel drug design software and shares the 2008 Thomas Alva Edison Patent Award for the discovery of Sprycel, an anti-cancer drug. Novels: *Algorithm* (2010 RPLA) and *As Wings Unfurl* (Best Pre-Pub Sci-Fi 2014 RPLA). Anthology: *My Shorts* (13 short stories, pub 2017). His latest manuscript, Wind-In-Trees (winner of a 2016 RPLA) is currently represented by Stephanie Hanson of Metamorphosis Literary Agency, and is about the last human, a Lakota Sioux, facing an apocalyptic invasion. Many of Arthur's short stories have garnered awards, including Honorable Mentions in the L. Ron Hubbard Writers of the Future Competition. He is also an award-winning artist (oil and graphics) who has published book covers and internal illustrations.

Douglas Anstruther was raised among the long cold winters of Minnesota. At age seven, he discovered that there were other worlds beyond our own, and was astonished—and disappointed—that no one had thought this important enough to mention earlier. A sentiment he still holds today. At some point, he married his lovely wife, Dana, went to medical school, had three nearly perfect children, and moved to Wilmington, North Carolina. When not tending to people's kidneys, Douglas likes to read, write, and talk about history, linguistics, space, AIs, the singularity, and everything in between. He enjoys writing stories that will rattle around in the readers' head for a while after the last page has been turned.

E. M. Eastick was born and raised in northern Australia. She traveled and worked as an environmental professional in Britain, Ireland, and the United Arab Emirates, before becoming a writer of no-fixed genre. Her creative efforts can be found in dozens of anthologies and magazines, including the 13th Annual Writer's Digest Short Story Competition, where "The Soap Maker" placed among the top ten winners. After living in Colorado for many years, E. M. recently returned to Australia, where she hopes to complete a co-written YA fantasy trilogy. Her short stories can be found on Amazon and Goodreads, under *E. M. Eastick.*

Ellen Denton is a freelance writer living in the Rocky Mountains, with her husband and three demonic cats who wreak havoc and hell (the cats, not the husband). Her writing has been published in over a hundred magazines and anthologies. She has also had an exciting life working as a rodeo clown, a nuclear physicist, and an exotic dancer in the crew lounge of the starship Enterprise. She was also the first person to scale Mount Everest to its summit. (Writer's note: The one-hundred-plus publication credits are true, but some, or all, of the other stuff may be fictional.)

Gregory D. Little is the author of the *Unwilling Souls* series, set in a world where technology is powered by the souls of the dead, the gods are locked away in the hollowed-out center of the planet, and what remains of humanity has rebuilt its cities out of the corpses of the great beasts that destroyed them. His short fiction can also be found in the *A Game of Horns*, *Dragon Writers*, and *Undercurrents* anthologies. He writes the kind of stories he likes to read—fantasy and science fiction tales featuring vivid worlds, strong characters, and smart action, all surrounding a core of mystery. He lives with his wife and their Labrador retriever.

Robin Pond is a Toronto-based playwright and fiction writer. His plays, mainly comedies, have received hundreds of performances, and publication with Eldridge and YouthPLAYS and in numerous anthologies. Robin's mystery novel, *Last Voyage*, was published as an e-book in 2018. As well as "Quantum Entanglement," Robin also has a second science-fiction story, "Close Encounter," being published in 2019, and a third, "Missing," is currently shortlisted.

Jon Wesick is a regional editor of the *San Diego Poetry Annual*. He's published hundreds of poems and stories in journals such as the *Atlanta Review*, *Berkeley Fiction Review*, *Metal Scratches*, *Pearl*, *Slipstream*, *Space and Time*, *Tales of the Talisman*, and *Zahir*. The editors of *Knot Magazine* nominated his story "The Visitor" for a Pushcart Prize. His poem "Meditation Instruction" won the Editor's Choice Award in the 2016 Spirit First Contest. Another poem "Bread and Circuses" won second place in the 2007 African American Writers and Artists Contest. "Richard Feynman's Commute" shared third place in the 2017 Rhysling Award's short poem category. Jon is the author of the poetry collection *Words of Power, Dances of Freedom*, as well as several novels, and most recently the short story collection *The Alchemist's Grandson Changes His Name*. JonWesick.com

Teresa Trent loves creating small towns filled with quirky characters and high crime rates. She started writing the Pecan Bayou Mystery Series in 2011, and adds to it yearly. She also writes the Piney Woods Mystery Series, published by Camel Press, which debuted in 2018. Teresa lives in Houston, Texas, with her family and spends her time as a writer and caregiver. Visit her website, TeresaTrent.com.

Terry Sanville lives in San Luis Obispo, California, with his artist-poet wife (his in-house editor) and two plump cats (his in-house critics). He writes full-time, producing short stories, essays, poems, and novels. Since 2005, his short stories have been accepted more than three hundred fifty times by commercial and academic journals, magazines, and anthologies, including *The Potomac Review*, *The Bryant Literary Review*, and *Shenandoah*. He was nominated twice for Pushcart Prizes, and once for inclusion in the *Best of the Net* anthology. His stories have been listed among The Most Popular Contemporary Fiction of 2017 by *The Saturday Evening Post*. Terry is a retired urban planner and an accomplished jazz and blues guitarist—who once played with a symphony orchestra backing up jazz legend George Shearing.

Tom Jolly is a retired astronautical/electrical engineer who now spends his time writing sci-fi and fantasy, designing board games, and creating obnoxious puzzles. His stories have appeared in *Analog SF*, *Daily Science Fiction*, *Compelling Science Fiction*, *New Myths*, and a number of anthologies, including *As Told By Things* and *Shards*. He lives in Santa Maria, California, with his wife, Penny, in a place where mountain lions and black bears still visit. You can discover more of his stories at www.silcom.com/~tomjolly/tomjolly2.htm.